FROM THE NANCY DREW FILES

THE CASE: Run a check on Brenda Carlton's newest heartthrob—a handsome entertainer with a shadowy past.

CONTACT: Frazier Carlton. The newspaper publisher, worried about his daughter, has Nancy dig into Mike McKeever's past—and she finds plenty of dirt.

SUSPECTS: Mike McKeever—*the gorgeous singer may be a hardened criminal.*

Felix Frankson—*the mysterious bearded man keeps turning up at all the wrong times.*

Chief Saunders—*the law officer seems very reluctant to investigate what really happened to Darla DeCamp.*

COMPLICATIONS: Mike McKeever seems to have a crush on Nancy, bringing out the worst in Brenda—and giving Ned a jealousy problem.

Books in THE NANCY DREW FILES® Series

Available from ARCHWAY paperbacks

THE NANCY DREW FILES™ CASE • 22

FATAL ATTRACTION

Carolyn Keene

AN ARCHWAY PAPERBACK
Published by POCKET BOOKS
New York   London   Toronto   Sydney   Tokyo

AN ARCHWAY PAPERBACK *Original*

An Archway Paperback published by
POCKET BOOKS, a division of Simon & Schuster Inc.
1230 Avenue of the Americas, New York, NY 10020

ISBN: 0-671-68730-1

First Archway Paperback printing April 1988

10 9 8 7 6 5 4 3 2

FATAL ATTRACTION

Chapter

One

Heads up, Bess!" George Fayne shouted, batting the ball.

"Hey, George, not so hard!" Bess Marvin yelled back. "We all *know* you're a natural athlete. You don't have to prove it with every shot!"

George, lean and tanned in her white bikini, grinned teasingly at Bess. "Do you think you could try to *hit* the volleyball, instead of worrying about breaking a fingernail?"

On the other side of the net, Ned Nickerson laughed. "I thought you guys were going to beat me, hands down. So what's happened to your game?"

Nancy leaned back onto the beach blanket, her new blue bikini bright against the pale green cloth. The lake was calm, the sun warm, and she felt very lazy. She took another sip of root beer as her eyes followed the volleyball back and forth across the net. They'd *all* been playing until a few minutes ago, when Ned had challenged George and Bess to a game and was now wiping them out because Bess had dropped every other ball.

Nancy smoothed suntan lotion on her arms, smiling to herself. They'd driven up from River Heights just last night, Thursday night, but already it promised to be a great weekend. They were staying in a borrowed lakefront vacation house just a stone's throw from the beach, and there was going to be plenty of time for relaxing. In the last few months she'd had one tough case after another, as word of her talent for solving impossible mysteries was rapidly spreading. But the last case, *Recipe for Murder,* had been one of the toughest, for she'd been up against clever, international spies. After that, Nancy was glad to take a breather from detective work—and from volleyball—even if it was just a short one.

Bess cupped her hands and called, "Hey, Nancy, why don't you come on back to the game? If we had you, we could beat the Incredible Hunk." She flipped her blond hair over her shoulder and brushed the sand off her green swimsuit. It looked great, and she swore she felt five pounds slimmer in it—which was vitally important to Bess, since she was always worried about being five pounds overweight.

Nancy shook her head and lay down, pushing her red-gold hair out of her eyes and adjusting her sunglasses. "Nope, I'm on vacation," she said, reaching for her novel. *This* vacation, she'd decided, she wasn't going to read a single mystery or work a single crossword puzzle. She was going to give her overworked brain a rest. *"Nothing* could tempt me to stir from this blanket."

"Miss Drew?"

Nancy blinked and sat up. Standing beside her was a man in a brown uniform with "Crown Courier" on the pocket. He had a letter in his hand.

"Yes, I'm Nancy Drew." Nancy glanced up toward the house. The delivery truck was parked in the driveway.

The courier handed her the letter. "I was going to leave this at the house, but then I saw you down here." He shoved his clipboard at her. "Sign, please."

With a resigned sigh, Nancy signed. The brown envelope had her name and the words "Urgent" and "Extremely Confidential" written on it. Without saying anything more, the courier trudged up the hill toward the road.

Nancy turned the letter over in her hand. There was an uneasy feeling in her stomach that told her it had to mean trouble. For a moment, she was tempted to stick the letter in her beach bag and forget about it until next week. But the only way to banish the worried feeling was to read the letter right away.

"What was *that* all about? Who was the guy in the uniform?" Ned Nickerson dropped down beside Nancy, drying his brown hair with a towel, his bronzed shoulders glistening with sweat.

"A courier," Nancy said. "He brought this letter." Intently, she read it through. "Nancy Drew," it said, "you are urgently needed to work on a *most* important and confidential case. Without your help, someone you know may be in serious trouble. It is imperative that you meet me at the HiPoint Drive-in Theater, at ten tonight. Come alone." Without a word, she held out the letter to Ned.

Ned whistled softly when he'd finished reading it. "Someone you know?" He looked at Bess and George, now horsing around at the edge of the lake. "You don't suppose . . ."

Nancy shook her head, her mouth set in a grim line. In the years she'd worked as a detective, there had been dozens of threats to her life—*and* to the lives of her friends. It was something she never took lightly. "I don't know," she said. "Maybe it's nothing. But I've got to find out."

Frowning, Ned looked down at the letter. "I guess this means you'll want to go back into River Heights tonight. But what about our vacation?"

Nancy made her voice light. "I'll just have to take a few hours off." She turned over onto her stomach. "Could you put some lotion on my back?" she asked in a muffled voice.

Ned poured some lotion into his hand and began to smooth it gently on her bare shoulders. After a minute he bent forward and kissed the tip of her ear. "How about if I drive you into River Heights tonight?" His voice was as soft and gentle as his fingertips.

Nancy sat up and leaned forward to kiss him back. "Thanks, Ned," she said, grateful for his help and his deep, enduring friendship. Things weren't always this comfortable between them. Ned sometimes felt that Nancy's detective work got in the way, and more than once he'd said that he just couldn't put up with it any longer. But she knew how terribly sad and empty her life would be without him and she hoped they would always be able to work out their differences, just as they had in the past.

"I'm worried about this meeting," Ned said thoughtfully, still rubbing Nancy's shoulders. "HiPoint Drive-in has been abandoned for years. It's not a good place to be, even *without* some mysterious stranger stalking around. Why do you suppose somebody would want to meet you there, of all places?"

"I don't know," Nancy said. "I might not take the risk if the letter didn't sound so threatening. If George or Bess is in danger—"

"Yeah, I know," Ned said. He dropped a kiss onto her shoulder. "Tell you what. I'll take you in to pick up your car, then follow you as far as HiPoint Road. When you're finished talking to whoever this is, you could meet me."

Nancy rolled over and touched Ned's face lightly. "Thanks, partner," she whispered. "I really appreciate the help."

"No charge," Ned said, gently brushing her lips with his.

"Hey, you two, you know the rules. No kissing in public!" George pulled a red beach towel out of her bag and sat down. She shook her curly dark hair vigorously, showering Nancy and Ned with a spray of water.

Bess plopped down on the sand. "Speaking of kissing in public"—she laughed—"you'll never guess who I ran into yesterday."

Nancy hurriedly shoved the letter into her beach bag. There was no point in alarming Bess and George until she knew the details of the threat. "Who?" she asked lazily, putting her sunglasses back on.

"Why, none other than ace reporter Brenda

Carlton, that's who," Bess said sarcastically. She reached for the suntan lotion.

"Kissing in public?" George hooted. "Whoever the guy is, somebody ought to cue him in to Brenda. She's an accident waiting to happen."

Nancy laughed. George had described Brenda Carlton to a *T*. She was always tooting her own horn about being the best investigative reporter at *Today's Times,* the award-winning newspaper owned by her father, Frazier Carlton. But Brenda's "investigations" always caused trouble.

"I don't know how you can laugh about it, Nan," Ned said, frowning. "She deliberately blew your cover when you were investigating that espionage case at Bedford High. And she managed to get you arrested on suspicion of murdering Mick Swanson, at *Flash* magazine. Remember?"

"Remember? How could I ever forget *darling* Brenda?" Nancy murmured, recalling the time Brenda challenged her to a detective duel to solve the Harrington case. Before it was over, she'd nearly gotten them both killed with her clumsy bungling.

"So what's this about Brenda kissing somebody in public?" George asked, lying back on the towel and pulling her straw hat over her face. "I want to hear more."

"Last night I went over to Charlie's," Bess told her, "that new place on the south side. They've got this great guitarist, just in from out of town. But Brenda got there first and staked her claim on him—and believe me, she was making the best of it. She was practically sitting in his lap." She sighed. "Too bad. He's really a hunk. A *gorgeous* hunk."

"Oh, yeah?" George asked, cocking up her hat. "Who *is* this guy?"

"Somebody named Mike McKeever."

Ned glanced out at the lake. "Hey, isn't it just about time for a swim?" he asked.

Bess nodded. "Yeah. Talking about Brenda Carlton makes me anxious. A swim would help me work it off."

Nancy jumped to her feet. Whatever the ominous letter meant, there was nothing she could do about it until tonight. "Well, we can't have Bess suffering from anxiety." She laughed. "Come on, Ned, let's race them!" With Ned close behind, she ran toward the water, leaving the letter behind.

Still, try as she might, she couldn't push the questions out of her mind. *Who* was in trouble? Was it one of her friends? And what kind of danger was she walking into tonight? She shivered in spite of the warm sun. There were dozens of things she'd rather be doing this evening than meeting an anonymous letter-writer after dark in a deserted drive-in movie.

* * *

Nancy parked under the single, feeble light at the drive-in theater and turned off the ignition. It was reassuring to know that Ned was parked only a few blocks away, waiting for her and worrying about her safety. "Be careful," he'd said when he took her to pick up her Mustang. "This could be dangerous."

Dangerous or not, the deserted theater was certainly spooky. It seemed to echo with the soundtracks of all the old horror movies she had ever seen. The place looked empty, and Nancy didn't see the other car—a sleek black Lincoln parked in the shadows of the tumbled-down concession stand—until she had scanned the lot carefully. She studied the car, frowning. Where had she seen it before? If it belonged to the person who had written the letter, why wasn't there any sign of life?

As she waited, goose bumps began to rise on her arms, and a shiver went across the back of her neck. Wow, this place *really* gives me the creeps, she thought. Maybe I'd better make sure I'm locked in. Without taking her eyes off the empty Lincoln, she reached over to lock the passenger door.

But it was too late. The door was already opening. A tall, shadowy figure slid into the seat beside her and wrapped one strong, black-gloved hand around her forearm. A man's rough, gravelly voice broke the silence.

"I assume that you've come alone, Nancy Drew. I wouldn't want anyone to see us together."

The gloved grip tightened. Then, softly, the mysterious stranger laughed—a harsh, frightening laugh.

Chapter

Two

NANCY STARTED. THAT voice—in a flash, she knew the identity of the mysterious figure. It was Frazier Carlton, editor of *Today's Times,* Brenda Carlton's father!

"Mr. Carlton?" Nancy asked.

The man glanced into the backseat. "You *are* alone, Miss Drew?"

"Of course," Nancy snapped, annoyed. "What's all this about? Why all the mystery? If you wanted to talk to me, wouldn't it have been simpler to meet for lunch somewhere?"

"It might be simpler," Mr. Carlton agreed calmly, "but somebody might have seen us together." He was wearing a dark jacket and a dark turtleneck sweater—obviously an outfit designed to fade into the shadows. "I must impress upon you the importance of keeping the details of this case absolutely secret. No one must know that we've talked, except for the people you might need to work with you on the case."

Nancy took a deep breath. "Maybe you'd better begin at the beginning," she suggested.

Mr. Carlton leaned back in the seat. "I suspect that my daughter," he said grimly, "is involved with somebody who may be after her money. I'm afraid she might be in for some serious trouble."

Brenda? So *that* was who the letter had referred to—George and Bess weren't in trouble at all. "That's terrific!" Nancy exclaimed. And then, embarrassed, added, "I mean, that's *terrible.* Where's your evidence?"

Mr. Carlton cleared his throat. "My daughter is a great reporter and a wonderful girl," he said slowly, "but she isn't exactly the world's best judge of character." He grinned ruefully. "Sometimes she . . . well, she doesn't look before she leaps. *This* time she's jumped into a relationship with somebody who really worries me."

"Oh," Nancy said, remembering what Bess had told them that morning. "Are you by any chance talking about the guitarist at Charlie's?"

Mr. Carlton looked surprised. "Gossip gets around fast, doesn't it?" He shook his head wearily. "Yes, that's the one," he went on. "McKeever, his name is. Mike McKeever. Brenda met him a while ago on vacation in Miami Beach. Seems he was playing in a clubdown there—and he followed her back here."

Nancy nodded. "I see." But the fact that Brenda's new boyfriend was a performer didn't automatically make him a bad guy. "But I *don't* see," she added, "what makes you think that he's after Brenda's money."

Mr. Carlton drew his dark eyebrows together in a way that reminded Nancy of Brenda. "I've been a newsman for almost forty years, Miss Drew. I've got what they call a 'nose for news.' I'm used to operating on blind hunches, and those hunches are usually right on the money."

"But a hunch—"

Mr. Carlton held up his hand. "This guy doesn't strike me as the kind who'd give up a well-paying job for love. And that's exactly what he did when he followed Brenda back here. Charlie's doesn't pay a living wage, and Brenda's paying for all their dates. Furthermore, he got really angry when I asked an innocent question about his family. And when I tried to trace the license plates on his motorcycle, I found out that the bike they were from had been junked. He's driving on phony plates. I have a feeling—a father's intuition, maybe—that this attraction of

Brenda's will come to a bad end." A note of deep concern had crept into his authoritative voice. "And I'm convinced that *you're* the only one who can help her!"

"Me? Help Brenda? Not a chance." Nancy shook her head firmly. "You know, Mr. Carlton, that Brenda and I aren't exactly the best of friends. She would never accept—"

"I understand that," Mr. Carlton said urgently. "And if I'm wrong, Brenda must never know that we've talked! If she thought I hired you to investigate her boyfriend, she'd never speak to me again!"

Nancy thought of all the times she'd vowed to close Brenda's reporter's notebook for good. And bumbling Brenda was dangerous enough when she was on the periphery of a case—what would it be like with her right in the middle of one? But still, Nancy had never wanted her to get *hurt*. And Mr. Carlton was obviously very worried, to have gone to all this trouble.

"Let's get this straight," Nancy said. "You want me to protect Brenda from herself—and from this guy, if he's what you think he is. Is that right?"

Mr. Carlton nodded. "That's it exactly."

Nancy laughed a little. "Considering how impulsive Brenda is, I'd say that's a pretty big order."

"That's why *you're* the only one who can handle it," Mr. Carlton said, looking at her intently.

Nancy nodded. Mr. Carlton was right. It certainly wasn't her standard assignment. It would definitely be a challenge. But maybe that was exactly why it appealed to her.

"I probably ought to have my head examined, Mr. Carlton," Nancy said, sighing, "but I'll take the case."

"I still think you've got to be crazy, getting involved with Brenda Carlton," Ned told Nancy as they parked outside Charlie's the next night. "She'll drive you bananas in about thirty seconds." He reached for Nancy's hand as they walked toward the club.

Nancy sighed. "I have the feeling I'm going to regret it," she said. "But I can't resist a good mystery, and Mr. Carlton is convinced that something funny's going on." She grinned. "Thanks for agreeing to help, Ned."

"The things I do for love," Ned replied with a laugh, opening the door for her. The small club was standing room only, and everybody's eyes were glued to a small stage in the corner, where a handsome young guy with dark, curly hair was perched on a stool, expertly playing a guitar. The room was filled with the sounds of jazzy blues, and everyone was listening intently, not saying a word. The audience was mostly young people —Nancy saw only one person who looked over fifty, a man with gray hair and a gray beard.

"Well, that's Mike McKeever," Ned said, pointing to the guitarist.

"No wonder Brenda's got a thing for him," Nancy said, half under her breath. Mike McKeever had a brooding, sultry look about him that spelled attraction. Then she saw Brenda, sitting alone at a table on the far side of the crowded room, watching the stage almost hungrily. She was dressed in a skintight white top and white slacks, and her dark hair cascaded dramatically around her shoulders. There was an intent gleam in her dark eyes as she tapped her plum-red fingernails against her glass.

Ned chuckled. "Looks like she's got it real bad for the guy. She can't take her eyes off him."

As he spoke, the music ended and people started to talk again. The performer put down his guitar and stood up. Nancy and Ned watched as he made his way through the shoulder-to-shoulder crowd to the corner where Brenda was waiting with a greedy smile. He bent down to whisper something into her ear. Her hand came up to his head, her fingers twisting in his dark hair as she pulled him toward her.

"I'd say you're right, Ned," Nancy agreed.

After a minute, the performer sat back and signaled a waiter, who brought a big pitcher of iced coffee and put it on the table.

"So how are you going to handle this?" Ned asked curiously.

Nancy made a face. "It's hard to lay plans where Brenda's concerned," she said. "Let's just start a casual conversation and see where it leads. I'm hoping we can find out something concrete about this guy's background." She and Ned began to thread their way through the crowd.

Brenda's smile evaporated when she saw Nancy. "Well, well, if it isn't Wonder Girl of River Heights," she said icily.

Mike McKeever looked up. Close up, Nancy could see that he was movie-star handsome, with light blue eyes and a broad, muscular chest. The sleeves of his blue shirt were rolled to his elbow, revealing tanned, strong arms.

"Hi," he said.

Nancy smiled her brightest smile. "We just *had* to tell you," she said, bubbling, "what a *terrific* performer you are." On the other side of the table, Brenda eyed her suspiciously.

"Right," Ned chimed in, following Nancy's cue. "Especially that last song. It was great."

Mike's blue eyes lit up. "You think so?" he said. "Hey, thanks a lot. Glad you liked it." He motioned to a seat. "Have a seat?" He turned to Brenda with a questioning look, and Brenda grudgingly introduced Nancy and Ned.

As Nancy sat down, she looked at Brenda. "You're really lucky," she said smoothly, "to be friends with an up-and-coming star, I mean."

Brenda looked surprised, then pleased. "We *have* been having a good time since we met in Florida," she boasted. She laughed and poured Mike another glass of iced coffee from the pitcher on the table. "Do you know that Mike came all the way from Miami just to be with me?"

"All the way from Miami," Nancy said, marveling. "I suppose you were playing in a club down there, too," she added, to Mike.

Brenda ran a possessive finger down Mike's bare arm. "Mike has played all over the country —and some places right around here. The Waterloo Inn in Batesville and the Sweet Corn Festival over in Silver Hills, for example. And dozens of other places." She gestured proudly at the crowd that surrounded them. "And look at the way he's packing them in here."

Nancy relaxed a little. Maybe it wasn't going to be as hard as she'd thought to get background information on this guy—as long as silly, conceited Brenda wanted to brag about him. But she would have to be careful. Brenda might get the idea that she had a romantic interest in Mike.

Mike nodded and smiled, sipping his coffee. "Yes," he said modestly, "I've come a long way from the little town where I grew up."

Behind her, somebody bumped Nancy's chair, but she was too intent to notice. She leaned forward, smiling at Mike. This was *too* easy! "And where was that?" she asked.

Brenda's eyes narrowed, and she began to fidget a little. Clearly, she wasn't pleased that Nancy was asking questions of her new prize.

"Oakton, Vermont," Mike said, obviously flattered by Nancy's interest. "It's just a wide place in the road, actually." The crowd around the table was getting noisier and Mike had to raise his voice to be heard.

"Well, River Heights isn't exactly the big city, either," Nancy said. "After the big city, it must be pretty quiet. Where are you staying?"

"The Ridgeview Motel," Mike said. Somebody walked between the tables and he leaned forward to avoid being jostled. "Out on Ridgeview Road. It's pretty much of a dump."

Brenda gave Nancy a dirty look. "But Mike won't always stay in dumps. Just wait until he hits the top of the charts." She lifted her chin. "Why, when he was playing in Miami Beach, a guy from Crescent Records happened to hear him and wanted him to—Hey, what's going on?"

Nancy looked down. Out of the crowd, a pair

of hands had gripped the edge of the table, right beside her elbow. The table lurched violently. The pitcher rocked a couple of times and then fell over with a crash, sending a stream of iced coffee cascading into Brenda's lap! Her furious screech filled the room.

Chapter

Three

Oooh!" Brenda jumped up, her face twisted with rage. A brown stain was spreading across the front of her white slacks. "Just see what that idiot did. He's ruined a brand-new pair of pants —and he did it on purpose! He *deliberately* tried to turn our table over!" She turned angrily to Mike. "Go after him, Mike! Show him he can't get away with it!"

Nancy turned to look. The man who had nearly dumped the table was the same grayhaired man she'd seen earlier. He was disappearing rapidly—and very determinedly—through the door.

Petulantly, Brenda stamped her foot. "What's wrong, Mike? Why don't you go after him?"

Nancy looked curiously at Mike. His face was flaming, and he was avoiding Brenda's angry eyes.

"Well, I, uh . . ." he muttered. He stood up. "I'll go tell the waiter to bring a mop."

"Tell you what, Brenda," Nancy said placatingly, "let's go to the rest room. A flight attendant taught me a secret for getting out coffee stains. All you need is club soda."

"Well, okay," Brenda said sullenly. She looked at Mike. "But I still don't understand why you didn't show that guy a thing or two. He *deliberately* dumped our table."

Nancy got some club soda from a waiter and followed Brenda into the rest room, where she sopped it on the wet stain, blotting it with a towel. After a minute, the brown began to fade.

"There," Nancy announced, straightening up. "After it's washed, you'll never know what happened. It'll be good as new."

Brenda tossed her black hair haughtily. "And what's *your* sudden interest in my business?" She paused and a mistrustful note came into her voice. "Have you got a thing for Mike McKeever?"

"Are you kidding?" Nancy asked. She took a deep breath. Brenda had an irritating way of making her lose her cool. But she couldn't afford to now. No matter how much she was tempted to lose her temper, she had to keep her wits and focus her attention on the case. "I mean," she said, in a calmer voice, "Ned Nickerson is more than enough for me. Why should I be interested in somebody else?"

"Then why were you coming on to Mike with all those questions?" Brenda growled, hands on hips.

In spite of herself, Nancy's temper flared. "I was just curious, that's all," she said, carefully keeping her voice even. Remember that you're on a case, Nancy, she told herself.

Brenda's mouth set into a taut line, her eyes blazing. "Curiosity can get you into a whole lot of trouble if you don't watch out." Her voice rose to a screech. "I warn you, Nancy Drew, stay away from this guy. He's mine, and I intend to keep him!"

There was a pounding on the door. "Hey, what's going on in there?" a girl's voice asked. "If you two are going to go at it, do it in the parking lot so other people can use the bathroom."

Brenda glared at Nancy. "You just remember what I said," she hissed. "Stay away from Mike McKeever! Or you'll be very, *very* sorry."

"The more I think about it," Nancy said, "the sorrier I am—sorry that I took the case, that is." She took one last look in the picnic basket to make sure she'd put out on the picnic cloth all of the lunch Hannah Gruen, the Drews' housekeeper, had made. "You can say 'I told you so' if you want to, Ned."

"What I can't figure out," Ned said, taking a sandwich, "is why McKeever didn't say something to that gray-haired guy. Brenda was right —he *did* dump the table on purpose. I saw him."

Nancy nodded. "I wondered about that too," she said thoughtfully. "In fact, I thought Mike even looked guilty, like a little kid who'd been caught with his hand in the cookie jar. We'll have to file that away as something to think about." She helped herself to coleslaw. "Too bad you had to miss all the fireworks in the rest room." She laughed. "Brenda was really mad."

Ned chuckled. "I told you so," he said teasingly. "If you ask me, Brenda's the *real* problem on this case. From the looks of it, she's nuts about the guy. There's no telling what she might do if she thinks you're meddling in her love life."

Nancy made a face, remembering Brenda's threat. "True. Well, anyway, I guess I've got my work cut out for me. Now that we know that Mike's from Oakton, Vermont, I'll start there, to get a line on his family and check his birth records. Even though we don't have his date of birth, it's a small town, and we're bound to find out something. And I think I'll give Dirk Bowman a call, in Fort Lauderdale."

"Isn't he a detective?"

"Right." Nancy smiled, remembering Dirk, with his sandy hair and quick smile. She had met him when she and Bess and George had gone to sunny Fort Lauderdale for vacation and found themselves on a hit-and-run holiday. She had helped Dirk wind up the case he was on, and he'd probably be glad to help her out on this one. "If McKeever's been up to anything fishy in Fort Lauderdale," Nancy added, "Dirk will know about it."

Early Monday morning Nancy put in a call to Oakton, Vermont. The town clerk, a woman, had a flat Vermont twang. "The name doesn't ring a bell with me," she said when Nancy gave her Mike's name and the approximate year of his birth. "And I've worked here for eighteen years. But I'll see what I can dig up and call you back."

Nancy set the receiver in its cradle, then picked it up again quickly and dialed another number. On the other end, the phone rang twice before Nancy heard a voice say, "Fort Lauderdale police."

"Dirk Bowman, please," Nancy said. "Tell him Nancy Drew is calling."

As she waited, Nancy smiled softly, imagining Dirk's friendly smile and the dimple that flashed in his cheek. They had great respect for each other's ability, and they'd become good friends on the case they'd worked on together. From the sound of Dirk's warm response when he came on the line, his memories were just as pleasant as hers.

"It's great to hear from you, Nan! Been solving any exciting crimes lately?"

"Oh, one or two." Nancy laughed. "In fact, I'm on a case now. That's why I'm calling. I think you can help. I'm trying to get the story on a musician named Mike McKeever. He used to play at the coffeehouses in Lauderdale, and I thought you guys might have something on him. I'd sure like to hear about it if you do."

"No problem. If he's left any dirty laundry here, we'll find it. But in order to get a positive on him, I'll need a clear photo and a set of prints, if you can get them."

"That shouldn't be too hard," Nancy said. "Maybe I can get a publicity shot from the club he's playing at now. How do you want me to send it?"

"Why don't you find a facsimile machine and put it on the wire?" Dirk suggested. "Just give me a call and let me know when so I can look for it." His voice dropped a little. "And watch yourself, detective." Then Dirk's tone lightened up, the worried sound slipping away. "You know, it would really be great to see you again."

"Thanks, Dirk. Maybe we'll get that chance sometime. Oh, and Dirk . . . thanks." Gently, she replaced the receiver, smiling. It *had* been fun, working with a real cop in Fort Lauderdale.

Nancy's thought was broken by the jangling ring of the phone. She grabbed the receiver before the second ring. "Hello," she said.

"Hello, this is the Oakton Town Office," the clerk said. "I've got some information on the person you were asking about."

"Good." Nancy took out her pencil. "Shoot."

"We *do* have a birth record for a Michael McKeever, born here to Mr. and Mrs. Alexander McKeever, on July eighteenth, twenty years ago."

With a sense of elation, Nancy hurriedly jotted down the information. This would make it a lot easier to do a complete check on Mike's background. "Is that all you've got?" she asked.

"Not quite," the clerk said slowly. "You see, we also have a *death* certificate, filed on July twenty-third, that same year. Michael McKeever died when he was just five days old!"

Chapter

Four

Dıᴇᴅ!" Nᴀɴᴄʏ ᴇxᴄʟᴀɪᴍᴇᴅ, her heart doing a somersault. "But that's not possible! I met him just yesterday. And he was *very* much alive!"

"But it's true," the clerk insisted. "I'm holding a copy of the death certificate."

"Is there any way to explain something like this?" Nancy wanted to know. There had to be a mistake, she told herself. Or . . . or maybe it was something *more* than a mistake. Maybe the *real* Mike McKeever *had* died twenty years ago and the man who was dating Brenda Carlton was a fake.

"Unfortunately, it's not hard to get a new birth

certificate—and a new identity," the clerk said with a sigh. "All someone has to do is say that the original birth certificate is lost, then give us the name and the birth date of someone who died as an infant. Since we don't routinely check death records against these requests, we usually issue the new certificate, believing that we're issuing a legitimate duplicate. The imposter can use it to get a social security card and a driver's license. It's a real racket—some people are even in the business of *selling* identities."

"Thanks," Nancy said, "I think." She hung up. So Mike McKeever wasn't the *real* name of Brenda's sexy new boyfriend! This was the first concrete evidence she'd found to support Mr. Carlton's hunch that Mike—or whoever he was —wasn't up to any good. You didn't go to the trouble of changing your identity for the fun of it. You only did it when you had something to hide. What was Mike hiding?

Nancy doodled on her note pad. She'd found herself up a blind alley with her first inquiry, but there was a good chance that Dirk Bowman could help her get a lead on Mike's true identity. She would need a picture and a set of prints. She reached for her purse and her car keys. Maybe Charlie's would have an extra publicity photo of their star performer.

In ten minutes, Nancy was back at Charlie's, which was almost empty at this time of the day.

The club's bald-headed manager was in his office.

"A publicity photo?" the manager asked, in response to her question. "Yes, I think so. In fact, I remember filing it last week. We're planning to run it in the paper next weekend." He went to a file cabinet and opened a drawer. "Here it is."

But the file was empty. "That's strange," he said, staring at it. "I would have sworn—"

"Could somebody have taken it?"

"Maybe." The manager shook his head wearily. "There's a black-haired girl who hangs out here all the time. She's really fallen for him. Maybe she took it."

Nancy frowned, considering. Could Brenda have stolen the photo to put up on her wall? That didn't make sense—Brenda could *take* a snapshot of Mike if she wanted one. Maybe Mike himself had taken the photo—but why?

There weren't any answers to these questions just now, and Nancy had to concentrate on getting another photo. And for *that,* she needed to find Mike McKeever and convince him to pose for her. Maybe she ought to make a trip out to the Ridgeview Motel, where he was staying.

Nancy didn't have to drive all the way out to the motel after all. She was leaving Charlie's when she unexpectedly bumped into him.

"Hi, Mike," she said, smiling up at him. Really, she thought to herself, it isn't too hard to *act* as though I think he's cute. Mike McKeever, Mystery Man, is one good-looking guy. But he's got a secret to hide. Until I know what that secret is, and whether or not there's a real crime involved here, I've got to be very, very careful with him.

Mike looked at her appreciatively. "Hi, Nancy," he said.

"How about joining me for a soda?" Nancy asked. "I'm dying to hear more about your performing career." If he handled a glass, maybe she could sneak it into her purse and lift the prints later.

Mike looked around. "Well, I don't know if I have time," he said a little nervously. "I mean, I just came to pick up my check and I'm supposed to meet somebody. . . ."

"Oh, Brenda?"

"Uh, no," Mike said uncomfortably, "not Brenda."

Who *was* he meeting? Nancy wondered. But it wasn't something she could pursue at the moment—she had another, more urgent job to do.

"Well, then," Nancy said. "I wonder if you'd do me a favor." Without waiting for an answer, she hurried on, inventing as she went. "I did some work for *Flash* magazine a while back, and I got to know the editors pretty well. They're interested in buying photographs of promising performers. You're *so* photogenic—I think they'd really jump at the chance to do a photo feature on you. But I'd need to send them a couple of shots so they could get a look at you."

Mike's face relaxed a little. "You really think they'd be interested?" he asked hopefully. "Gee, that would give my career a terrific boost! Maybe then I'd finally be able to get away from—" He stopped. "That would be great."

"Let me just run out to my car for my camera," Nancy suggested. "Listen, let's make this a really relaxed pose, with you sitting at a table with a glass in your hand. Why don't you get something to drink while I'm gone?" If she did this right, she thought as she dashed to her car and got the camera out of the glove compartment, she could get both the picture *and* the prints at one time.

In a minute she was back, and had posed Mike at a table on the terrace, a glass in his hand.

"That's perfect!" she said, clicking the camera. "Turn your head just a little—there!" She took two more pictures. She would send all of them to Dirk, just to be sure he could get a positive identification.

Mike glanced at his watch and drained his glass quickly. "Listen, I've got to go. I sure hope that *Flash* likes the pictures."

"Oh, I'm sure they'll *love* them," Nancy said, keeping her eye on Mike's empty glass. All she had to do was wait until he'd turned to go, slip the glass into her purse, and—

"You through with this?" the waitress asked, coming up with a tray.

Mike nodded. The waitress scooped up the glass and Mike stood up.

"See you later, huh?" he said, and walked to a motorcycle parked in the lot. Nancy was left staring at the waitress. Should she try to rescue the glass? No, she couldn't be sure now which one it was, of the half dozen on the tray. Great, she thought disgustedly. Now she'd have to look for another way to get the fingerprints. But she had the pictures, and that was what really mattered.

Nancy got into her Mustang and put the camera into her glove compartment. It wasn't noon yet—if she dropped the film off at the photo lab downtown, she could get the photos back in a couple of hours and put them on the wire to Dirk this afternoon.

As Nancy drove by McBride's Drugs, she screeched to a stop. There were a few things she needed to pick up, and she wouldn't be passing any drugstores on her way home from the lab. It'll just take a minute, she told herself as she got out of the car and stuck her keys in her pocket.

When she returned, she was surprised at how warm the car had gotten in such a short time. It was probably a good idea to take the camera from the glove compartment and put it someplace cooler.

Nancy felt around inside the cluttered glove compartment. Where *was* that camera, anyway? She pulled out a few maps, some old napkins, an empty pack of gum.

A sick feeling twisted inside her stomach. The camera—with the precious pictures of Mike —was gone. The glove compartment was empty!

For a moment, Nancy just stared at the empty glove compartment, stunned—and then angry— at her carelessness in leaving the car unlocked. But how could she have known someone would act so quickly?

Nancy sat back in the seat, biting her lip, remembering that the publicity photos had been stolen from Charlie's. There was a distinct possibility that the thief had been watching her earlier. And there was also the possibility—maybe even a *probability*—that the thief was someone who wanted the film, and not the camera. Could it have been Mike himself? Doubtful. He'd obviously been intrigued with the idea of *Flash* magazine doing a feature on him. What was it he'd said? Something about finally being able to get away? Get away from what?

Nancy didn't have time to pursue this line of thinking any further. A tomato-red car breezed past. The driver was looking straight ahead, but Nancy didn't need to be a detective to recognize the vehicle and the driver's long black hair. So Brenda Carlton was in the neighborhood! Had *she* been at Charlie's, too, and spotted Nancy and Mike? Had she decided to steal the camera as a signal to Nancy to stay away from Mike?

Nancy shook her head. It was possible—but not very likely. She knew that if Brenda wanted the pictures, she wouldn't steal the camera. She'd make a noisy scene, demanding that Nancy return the film. No, much as she hated to admit it, she was sure that Brenda wasn't the thief.

Now that her plan to get a picture had been blown, Nancy knew she had to come up with an alternative quickly. But she couldn't count on being able to con Mike into posing again. She slumped down in the car seat, frowning. How *was* she going to get that photo?

"So you want *us* to make like groupies and take Mike's picture," George said from the back seat of Ned's car. The four of them—Nancy, Ned, Bess, and George—were on their way to the club later that night, after Nancy had filled them in on the details of the case.

Beside George, Bess smiled dreamily, adjusting the collar of her brand-new blue blouse. "Maybe we can make it a close-up," she suggested, "with *me.*"

"A close-up would be great," Nancy said with a grin. She leaned over the front seat. "In fact, if you sat beside the stage and pretended to be a couple of ardent fans, you could whip out your camera and—"

"You're sure that Mike McKeever isn't going to object?" George asked cautiously. "I don't want anything to happen to *my* camera."

"That's what *we're* here for," Ned reminded George, pulling into the lot and parking. "We won't go in, because it might blow your cover. But we'll be out here if you need us."

"Wish us luck," Bess said as they got out of the car. To George, she added, "Do you suppose he'll sign an autograph for me?"

"How long do you think this is going to take?" Ned asked after the two had disappeared into the club. They were parked under a single bright security light that lit the entire parking lot. It had been drizzling, and the rain made a halo around the light.

Nancy shrugged. "Not too long," she said. She stretched. "Unless Bess gets starry-eyed over Mike and forgets why they came."

"Well, then, we could have a lot of time, couldn't we?" Ned laughed. "Maybe it's *our* turn to do close-ups." He put both hands on her shoulders and pulled her close, gently, his lips touching hers. "Perfect," he sighed. "Now, if only somebody would cut that light—"

Almost by magic, the light went off, and the parking lot was shrouded in drizzly darkness.

"How'd you do that, Ned?" Nancy asked.

"Wishful thinking." Ned kissed her again.

With a happy sigh, Nancy gave herself up to Ned's kiss and the comforting circle of his strong arms. All she could feel was the warmth of his lips on hers; all she could hear was her own heart thudding in her ears.

Then, suddenly, it wasn't just her heart she was hearing. Out in the dark parking lot, there was a long, shrill scream that sent shivers up Nancy's spine. She and Ned looked up and saw a tangle of shadowy figures, struggling. Quickly, Ned flipped on the headlights. The bright beams bathed the struggling figures in light. Nancy could make out a bright blue blouse.

"It's George and Bess!" she exclaimed frantically. "They're being attacked!"

Chapter

Five

L ET'S GO!" NED shouted, shoving open the car door and jumping out. Nancy was right behind him as the two of them raced across the wet asphalt toward the tangle of struggling bodies. In the eerie illumination of the headlights, Nancy saw with a gasp that the short, stocky attacker had the wizened, hideously distorted face of a mummy. Then she realized it was only a Halloween mask, and she let out her breath. She saw the attacker yank the camera as George tried to wrestle it away from him.

Ned lunged into the assailant as hard as he could, knocking the man onto the wet pavement.

Nancy darted forward to snatch off the mummy mask. She saw that the man had gray hair and a short-clipped gray beard.

"Grab him, Nancy!" Bess screamed.

But Nancy was off-balance, and the attacker rolled away from her and scrambled to his feet. He ran a few yards, to an old green car parked in the shadows. The engine roared to life and the car sped away, tires screeching.

"Sorry," Ned said. "That push should have stopped a horse."

"At least we got this," Nancy said, picking George's camera up off the pavement.

"And *I* got this," Bess moaned, putting a hand to her face. A long scratch ran across her cheek. "Am I bleeding?"

"It's not too bad," Nancy said, examining it tenderly. "We'll get you home and put some iodine on it." She turned to George. "How about you?"

"Some bodyguards you two turned out to be." George held her hand to her eye with a rueful grin. "I think I'm going to have a black eye."

Nancy thought guiltily of the fun she and Ned had been having when they should have been watching for George and Bess. "I'm sorry," she said. "I just didn't expect—"

"I know," George broke in. "I didn't either. He jumped out of the shadows." She looked around. "That's funny—wasn't there a security light?"

Ned nodded. "It went out a few minutes ago. Whoever jumped you must've cut the power to the light so he could do his dirty work in the dark."

"That means he must know his way around Charlie's," Nancy said. "The switch box is probably inside somewhere."

"An employee, maybe?" George asked.

"Wouldn't it be a good idea if we discussed this in the car?" Bess asked plaintively. "We're getting *wetter.*"

"You know," Nancy said as all four of them started back toward Ned's car, "I've got the feeling that I've seen that guy before. Short, stocky, with a gray beard—" Suddenly she snapped her fingers. "I've got it!" she exclaimed. "It's the guy who dumped our table and spilled coffee all over Brenda!"

Ned stared at her. "Hey, you're right," he said. "Maybe he's making a career out of crashing people's parties."

"Yeah, maybe," Nancy said grimly. "But he's connected with this mystery somehow. Since he was so anxious to keep us from getting a picture of Mike, I'll bet he's the same guy who broke into my car and stole the camera. And took the publicity photo out of the file cabinet, too!" She shook her head in puzzlement. But what was his motive? And how was he tied to Mike McKeever?

"So you're up to your eyebrows in bad guys again, eh?" Carson Drew asked, putting down his morning paper. "What's the crime?"

Nancy, dressed in khaki pants and a safari shirt, sat down at the breakfast table and helped herself to Hannah's pancakes. "I wish I knew," she said. "And right now, I don't know what all these things are leading up to." She told her father briefly about the case.

"So what's your next step?"

"Getting some film developed. Then Bess and George and I are going on a reconnaissance mission to pick up a set of fingerprints."

Carson Drew folded the paper and pushed back his chair. "Well, I'm sure you'll be able to pull it off," he said with cheerful confidence. He bent over and kissed his daughter. "Be careful while I'm away in New York, Nancy. I want to find you in one piece when I get back."

Nancy grinned. Her father, who was used to dealing with criminals in his law practice, knew exactly what kind of dangerous scrapes she sometimes got herself into.

"I will," she promised. She finished her pancakes hurriedly, then went to the phone. It was after nine. Mr. Carlton ought to be in his office by now.

"I'm not surprised," Mr. Carlton growled when Nancy had told him about Mike's false identity. "But I'm afraid that the fact that this guy is using a phony name isn't going to be enough to convince Brenda to drop him."

Nancy nodded. If Brenda sensed *any* pressure from her father to drop Mike, she would become even more stubborn about him.

"Right," she agreed. "But there's something else, too—or maybe I should say *someone* else. This gray-haired man—he's connected to the case somehow. When we've figured out what that connection is, we'll know a whole lot more."

After she said goodbye and hung up, she took the film out of the safe in the den and tucked it into her purse. She'd been relieved last night to discover that the film hadn't gotten wet. *That* would have been a real disappointment, after all the trouble they'd had getting the pictures.

An hour later, Nancy had already dropped the film off at the photo lab and was heading toward the Ridgeview Motel with George and Bess.

"Ooh," George groaned, leaning over to look at herself in Nancy's rearview mirror. "Not only does this black eye *look* awful, but it hurts every time I blink!" She dabbed at the green and purple bruise that her makeup barely covered.

"So what's the game plan?" Bess asked. Her scratch was already beginning to heal.

"We're going to the Ridgeview Motel," Nancy told them. "To search Mike's room."

"What are we looking for?" Bess asked.

"Fingerprints—and anything else we can find," Nancy said. "We're really short of clues in this case. Not only that, but we're short of the real *crime,* when you get right down to it. We know that Mike McKeever definitely isn't who he says he is. But we've got no reason to think he's a criminal."

She pulled up in front of Mason's Office Supply, around the corner from the motel. There was a pay phone directly in front of them.

"Wait here a minute," Nancy instructed her friends. "I'm going to call Mike. If there's no answer, we'll assume the coast is clear."

In a moment she was back. "Okay, come on," she said. "He's gone."

Mike's room was on the second floor of the cheap, run-down motel. The locked door, with a window next to it, opened onto a long balcony that ran in front of all the rooms. Near the stairs, they found a maid's pushcart, loaded with cleaning supplies and dirty linen.

"Tell you what," Nancy told Bess, "why don't you get that cart and park it in front of the door. It'll be a good cover for us."

With the cart partially shielding her from view, Nancy took out her lockpick kit and stealthily set to work. Seconds later, the lock clicked, the cylinder turned, and she pushed the door open. Leaving Bess standing guard, she and George went in.

The room held a queen-size bed, blankets tossed back, a scratched dresser with a TV set on it, and a small table. The carpet had a musty smell, as if it hadn't been well vacuumed. A cheap picture hung crookedly on one wall.

Nancy pointed to the unmade bed. "The maid hasn't cleaned yet, so we'll have a better chance of getting some prints." She gestured toward the closet, where a half-dozen shirts and jackets hung untidily. "Why don't you search those clothes, George. But hurry. I don't want to be here any longer than we have to, in case Mike comes back."

While George was hastily going through Mike's pockets, Nancy looked around. On the table there was an empty glass. Good—maybe it would yield the fingerprints she needed. Quickly, she dusted it for prints, realizing with disappointment that she wasn't going to get much. There was only one print, a thumbprint. She transferred it with fingerprint tape onto an index card and slid the card into an envelope.

She turned to go into the bathroom. The faucet would be a good source of prints. "What are you finding?" she asked George.

"Not a lot," George said. "Just this ticket stub—no, wait, here's something else." She handed Nancy a ticket stub and a folded-over piece of pink notepaper.

Nancy opened the note. The script was feminine, the *i*'s dotted with little circles. The faint smell of floral perfume clung to it.

"Dear Mike," she read. "I just have to tell you how much I miss you when we're not together, and how much I love you. I pray that we'll never, ever be separated from one another, just the way you promise. Love and kisses, Darla."

"Mmmm," George said, "so Brenda's not his *first* love."

"And not likely to be his last," Nancy added with a little shudder, "unless we do something about it. This could be more than just a simple love-'em-and-leave-'em scheme." She hated the idea of somebody going around collecting girlfriends like bumper stickers. It was almost enough to make her feel sorry for Brenda—and certainly for Darla, whoever she was. She glanced at the blue ticket stub George had handed her. It was from the Batesville County Fair.

"Didn't you say that Mike had a job in Batesville?" George asked.

Nancy nodded. "That's what Brenda told us." Carefully, she put both the love note and the ticket stub into her purse. "Listen, let me check the faucets for prints. I have a feeling we ought to get out of—"

"Pssst!" It was Bess, just outside the door. "Somebody's coming up the stairs."

"Quick," Nancy whispered, going to the door. "We can't let anybody see us!"

Bess was standing beside the cart. She had found a maid's cap, and she was just putting it on. "Jump in!" she whispered, gesturing toward the hamper. "Hurry up, before he gets here!"

With a mad leap, both Nancy and George jumped into the large hamper of dirty linen and pulled the sheets over their heads.

"I don't believe we're doing this," George said, in a muffled voice.

Surreptitiously, Nancy raised one corner of a sheet and peered out as Bess hurriedly lowered her head and pushed the cart—with her friends in it—past the man who was walking down the balcony.

Nancy held her breath, staring at the short, stocky man as they passed close enough to touch him. He had gray hair and a gray beard! It was the same man who had jumped George and Bess and tried to steal the camera!

Chapter

Six

NANCY BIT HER lip, praying they wouldn't be discovered. But to her relief, the man seemed intent on his own business. As Bess pulled the cart around the corner, he paused in front of Mike's room, took a key out of his pocket, opened the door, and went in. There it was—the connection she'd been looking for. The man had a key to Mike's room!

In a moment, Nancy and George were climbing out of the laundry cart.

"Whew, that was a close one," George said, pulling a dirty pillowcase off her head.

Bess took off the cap and turned to Nancy, her

eyes round. "Wasn't that the same man—" She swallowed.

Nancy nodded grimly. "Yeah," she said. "It was. It's a good thing you put that cap on. I don't think he recognized you."

George looked at them. "Recognized her?"

"Right," Nancy said. "The man who just went into Mike's room is the same person who tried to beat you guys up last night."

"Wow." George touched her black eye reverently. "I don't want to have anything more to do with *him*."

"What are we going to do?" Bess asked anxiously. "Did we get what we came for?"

"We got only one print," Nancy said. "But maybe that will be enough." She looked thoughtfully back along the balcony. It was deserted. The man was still in Mike's room.

"You two stay here," Nancy commanded, making up her mind. "Whistle if anybody comes. I'm going to have a look."

Nancy pressed against the wall beside the window and peered intently into the room. The man was sitting on the unmade bed, dialing the phone. But although the drapes were open, the window was closed, and Nancy couldn't hear a thing. Frustrated, she leaned farther forward, risking discovery. It was no use—she still couldn't hear anything. She could only see that the man's gray hair was thinning and he had a scar on one cheek.

Nancy was concentrating so hard that she almost didn't hear George's low, piercing whistle. When she did, she glanced behind her, over the balcony, just in time to see Brenda climb out of her red car and slam the door. She jumped back hurriedly and dashed around the corner, out of sight.

"What do you suppose *she's* here for?" Bess whispered.

"Guess." George giggled.

Careful not to be seen, Nancy looked around the corner. Brenda, wearing a sleeveless, tightly belted blue tank dress, was knocking confidently at the door. "Mike," she called in a low, honeyed voice. "Mike, it's me, Brenda."

The door opened. "Yeah?" The man's tone was abrupt. He was obviously angry at the interruption. "What do you want?"

"Oh, uh, pardon me," Brenda said, flustered. She cleared her throat and stepped back. "I must . . . I must have the wrong room. I . . . I'm looking for Mike McKeever."

"He's not here," the man said.

"Oh, well, uh, it's okay." Brenda shifted nervously. "I was just in the neighborhood, and I thought I'd drop in."

"Yeah. I'll tell him you were here." The door

49

shut in Brenda's face. Looking confused, Brenda went down the stairs, got into her car, and drove off.

After a few minutes, the door to Mike's room opened again and the gray-haired man stepped out, closing the door behind him. He hurried down the steps and climbed into an old green car parked in the lot.

"Come on," Nancy said as they watched him start the motor. "We're going to tail him!"

The three girls raced down the stairs and around the corner to Nancy's car. She started it up just as the man pulled out of the lot, onto Ridgeview in front of them.

"There he goes!" Nancy exclaimed. "Hey, that's a neat old car—a Buick, I think. We won't lose *him* easily."

Staying a few car lengths back, Nancy followed the green Buick as it drove quickly down Ridgeview. She'd gone about four blocks, hanging back in the traffic so that the driver wouldn't spot them, when she checked the rearview mirror —and found herself staring right at Brenda Carlton! Brenda's face was twisted into a mask of rage, and she was hunched furiously over the steering wheel. Her tomato-red car was hugging Nancy's bumper. Was she going to rear-end them?

Nancy speeded up slightly to keep Brenda

from hitting them. "Don't look now, gang," she said, "but we're being followed."

"It's Brenda!" Bess exclaimed, swiveling around. "Is she trying to hit us?"

"The Buick's making a left on Albert Drive," George reported, pointing. She took a quick look behind her. "Is Brenda tailing us, or him?"

"Let's hope she's after *us*," Nancy said, turning left. "Otherwise, she'll give us away, for sure. If we can stay between her and the green car long enough, maybe our target will show us where he's headed. Then we can shake Brenda."

The green car led them toward the main business district. It turned into the parking lot of the public library, and the driver got out and walked briskly toward the library.

"Great!" Nancy breathed a sigh of relief. "It doesn't look like he spotted us." As she drove past the library and on down the street, she glanced in her rearview mirror. Brenda was still tailing them, looking even angrier than before. "Now, let's lose Brenda!" She speeded up.

At that second, the stoplight just ahead turned yellow. Nancy stepped on the gas and squeaked through the light. Brenda, who was caught momentarily off guard by the Mustang's sudden speed, was left several car lengths behind. Still, she didn't hesitate. She accelerated, right through the red light.

"Hey, look!" George said triumphantly, watching Brenda through the back window. "There's a cop!" George pointed to a police car pulling out of the cross street, its red light flashing.

"That's one way to stop her!" Bess noted.

Nancy glanced back. The red car had pulled over to the curb, and the officer was out of his patrol car and strolling toward it. She was sure that Brenda's face was as red as her car.

"Beautiful!" cried George. "That was great driving, Nancy."

"I'd give a month's allowance to hear *that* conversation," Bess added.

Smiling, Nancy headed back to the library, where she parked on a side street.

"You know, that guy didn't exactly look like the intellectual type," Bess remarked as they got out of the car. "I wonder what he's looking for in the library."

"There's only one way to find out," Nancy replied. "But we'll have to stay out of sight. We were lucky he didn't recognize us at the motel. We don't want him to spot us now."

The man was at the main desk, talking to the librarian. Then he went to the reading room. While Nancy and the others watched from behind a bookshelf, he pulled several documents from a filing cabinet and took them to a table, where he pored over them. Then, with a satisfied look, he put the documents away and walked out.

When the man had gone, Nancy went up to the main desk. The librarian was a woman she had known ever since she started checking out mysteries by the dozen. Recently, though, she'd been too occupied with *real* mysteries to think much about fictional ones.

"Hello, Miss Howard," she said.

"Why, Nancy Drew," the librarian said. She put down the file cards she was checking and smiled at Nancy over gold-rimmed glasses. "Can I help you?"

"Well, maybe," Nancy told her. "Actually, I'm interested in the man who spoke to you about fifteen minutes ago. He looked familiar. I'm curious—what was he looking for?"

Miss Howard nodded. "Oh, yes, that one. I didn't get his name. He's a distant cousin of the Carltons, and he wanted to check on the family history. I suggested that he go to the River Heights Historical Society. But he wanted more current information, so I sent him to the files where we keep that data."

"What was he interested in?"

Miss Howard frowned. "That was the funny part. Usually when people are checking on their family trees, they're more interested in who their relatives are than in how much they make."

"So he was after *financial* information."

"That's right. I guess he found what he was looking for, since he didn't ask any more questions." She smiled, leaning forward. "Now," she said, "can I interest you in a good mystery?"

"Thanks," Nancy replied with a rueful grin. "I think I've already got one."

"Well," Nancy said as the girls hurried down the library steps, "it's beginning to look like we're on to something. Obviously, since this guy has a key to Mike's motel room, the two of them are connected. And we know that they're interested in Brenda for more than just her pretty face." She glanced at her watch. "It's nearly lunchtime. After lunch, I'll call Mr. Carlton and bring him up to date. We probably haven't got enough to persuade Brenda to break off with Mike, but we're getting close."

Bess grinned. "Did you say something about lunch?" she asked. "The Creekside Patio has terrific shrimp salads."

"Sounds good to me," Nancy said, taking her keys out of her purse. They came around the corner to the car.

"Nancy!" George yelped, jumping backward. She clutched Nancy's arm. "Look at your car!"

Nancy glanced up. What she saw stopped her in her tracks. Across the windshield of her car was scrawled an ugly message, in dark red letters.

STAY AWAY FROM MIKE MCKEEVER—OR ELSE!

Chapter

Seven

W**HAT IN THE** world—" Bess sputtered as they went up to the car.

Nancy touched the red stuff with a finger, then sniffed at it. "It's lipstick," she said grimly. "Who do we know that wears this particular shade of plum-red lipstick?"

George snapped her fingers. "Brenda Carlton, who else?"

Nancy nodded. "Right. After the cop nabbed her, she probably cruised around for a while, looking for us. Then when she spotted the car, she left us this little message."

"The question is," Bess said, energetically

scrubbing at the lipstick with a tissue, "how we get this stuff off. It smears into a gooey mess."

"Bess," Nancy suggested, "why don't you go over to the gas station on the corner and get a towel with some grease solvent on it?"

As Bess hurried off, Nancy opened the car door and sat down on the seat, staring at the letters. "This case is hard enough," she said wearily, "without Brenda sticking her nose into it. Her interference makes it tougher to figure out who's doing what."

Frowning, George sat down beside her. "You don't suppose that Brenda would actually do anything to hurt you, do you?" she asked. She gestured at the threatening message. "I mean, I know she's capable of making mischief, but would she do anything really dangerous?"

Nancy shook her head. "I don't think so," she said slowly. "But she could do something really stupid, without thinking about the consequences —to herself or to somebody else."

When Bess came back with the solvent-soaked rag, they scrubbed the windshield. "What a mess," Nancy said glumly as the lipstick began to come off. It took five minutes' hard work before the glass was clean again.

"All this running around has made me really hungry," said George. "How about heading for that lunch now?"

"Fine with me," Nancy agreed. "We need some time to decide our next move."

The Creekside Patio had a deck built out over a rippling creek. They chose a shaded table, and Nancy sat down with relief, enjoying the cool breeze.

"So where are we now?" George asked Nancy after the waiter had taken their orders.

"It's beginning to look to me," Nancy replied slowly, "like a con game with two players. I'm speculating now, because we don't have any proof, but it may be that Mike's just a decoy —you know, the guy with the fatal attraction, who lures the girl. He's certainly sexy enough. The guy we saw doing research on the Carlton financial holdings could be the brains behind the business."

That would make sense, Nancy thought. What was it that Mike had said when she'd suggested that maybe *Flash* magazine might be interested in a photo feature? He'd said, "Then I'd be able to get away from . . ." Maybe this line of work was getting distasteful to him.

"Hey, Nancy!"

Nancy looked up to see Ned striding toward her. With a welcoming smile, she moved her chair, making room.

"I was driving by and saw your car out front. How'd it go this morning?" he asked.

Bess smothered a giggle. "You mean, before or after they jumped into the dirty linen?"

"Or before or after Brenda got a traffic ticket?" George asked.

"Or before or after my windshield got smeared with lipstick?" Nancy added.

"It must have been an interesting morning," Ned said, grinning. But his face was serious when Nancy gave him a quick recap of the day's adventures, even a verbatim report of the love note they'd found in Mike's pocket. "It sounds to me," he said, frowning, "as if Brenda's gotten herself into a mess—a really slimy one."

Nancy thought about the love note. Who was Darla? Had she been one of Mike's victims in his game of rip-off love? Had she wakened one morning to the awful realization that Mike McKeever had never cared about her, never intended to make good his promises?

"You know," she said slowly, still thinking of Darla, "if Brenda weren't—well, if Brenda weren't *Brenda,* it would be easy to feel sorry for her. Thinking someone's in love with you and then finding out he was only using you for your money must be the worst." She shuddered. "We've just got to put a stop to it."

"I wish we knew who that guy called from Mike's room," George said thoughtfully.

"I think I know somebody who can help trace it," Nancy replied. She thought ahead to the afternoon. "I need to get the film and put the photo and the thumbprint on the wire to Dirk Bowman. I've got enough to keep me busy for the rest of the day." She glanced at Ned. "But we have to get something more concrete on this guy. Maybe you and I should make a trip tomorrow, Ned. Brenda told us that Mike's last job—before the one in Florida—was in Silver Hills. Remember?"

Ned nodded. "Right. So you're thinking of driving over there to check up on him? It's only a couple of hours."

"Are you free tomorrow?"

"My time is *your* time," Ned said grandly, with a big grin.

"Speaking of time," Bess said, with a glance at George, "Peterson's is having a one-day-only sale—today. How about it, George?"

George nodded. "I need some new running shoes. If you're *sure* you don't need us this afternoon," she said, turning to Nancy.

"I'm sure," Nancy said. "Listen, do you remember that red shirt I tried on the last time we were in Peterson's? If it's on sale, will you pick it up for me?"

After lunch, Nancy headed off to pick up the developed film. The photos were clear and sharp, exactly what Dirk would need to check Mike's ID. With the pictures tucked safely into her purse, she stopped at the phone company. There she talked to an old friend of her father's, Mr. Conrad, who was a supervisor.

"I wonder if you could trace a phone call for me," Nancy said. She had jotted down the number of the motel and the number of Mike's room. "The call was made from this number, about ten-thirty this morning. I'd like to find out the number the person was calling. Can that be done?"

"Sure, it can," Mr. Conrad said confidently. "No problem at all."

He sat down at a computer and began to enter the numbers Nancy had given him. Almost instantly, the screen was filled with a long listing of numbers.

"Here we are," Mr. Conrad said, pointing to a row of numbers. "The call was made to Batesville. Here, let me copy the number for you."

Nancy stared at the screen, her mind racing as she began to put the pieces together. They had found the ticket stub from the Batesville County Fair, and Brenda had said that Mike played there. The phone call was one more link to the town, which was only a three-hour drive from River Heights. When she and Ned finished in Silver Hills, Batesville ought to be next on their list.

Nancy stood up and took the slip of paper the

supervisor handed to her. "Thanks, Mr. Conrad. I appreciate your help."

"Nothing to it. Tell your dad hello for me, will you?"

Nancy got into her car and drove home quickly. It was already nearly four on the East Coast, and she wanted to catch Dirk Bowman before he left.

Dirk sounded pleased when Nancy told him about the picture and the thumbprint. "If we've got anything at all on this guy," he told her, "I'll pass it along to you. But there's a hitch. I've got to get to a meeting that's going to tie me up the rest of the day. How about putting the stuff on the wire at nine tomorrow morning? That way I'll be here to get the ball rolling."

"Great," Nancy said. She put down the phone and then picked it up again, to dial Mr. Carlton. He listened quietly while she reported the events of the morning. But when she got to the part about Brenda's visit to the motel, he made a sharp, unhappy noise. And when she told him about Brenda's ticket, and about the lipstick message on the windshield, he sounded almost angry.

"Sometimes I just don't understand my daughter," he growled disgustedly. "How anyone so bright could act so *dumb* . . ."

Nancy coughed. "I've got the feeling we're on

the right track," she said. "Tomorrow morning I need to send the photos and the print to Fort Lauderdale. Can you help?"

"Sure," Mr. Carlton said. "There's a facsimile machine in the copy room on the second floor of the *Times,* down the hall from my office. I'll tell my secretary that you'll be there to use it and she's to see that you're not disturbed." He hesitated, and then added cautiously, "But use the back stairs, just to be on the safe side."

"You're right," she agreed. "I wouldn't want to run into Brenda." To tell the truth, Brenda Carlton was the *last* person she wanted to see.

Wednesday morning, Nancy made her way up the back stairs of the *Times* building, looking over her shoulder to be sure that no one saw her. It was early enough that Brenda was probably still in bed, but she wasn't taking any chances. Mr. Carlton's secretary was expecting her. She led Nancy to the copy room and showed her how to operate the facsimile machine, only one of several pieces of copying equipment in the room.

"Mr. Carlton instructed me to wait outside and not let anybody else in," she said, going to the door. "If you need any help, just call me."

"Thanks," Nancy said, glancing at the machine, which looked like a combination copier and answering machine. "I think I can manage."

Nancy put the thumbprint into the machine

and turned it on, punching Dirk's telephone number on the keypad. The machine began to *whirr* quietly, and the print fed through the machine, while Dirk's telephone number and the word *transmitting* appeared on the digital display. Less than thirty seconds later, the print was completely transmitted to Fort Lauderdale, over fifteen hundred miles away. Next Nancy fed in the first two photos, one after the other.

Outside in the hallway there was a buzz of conversation. Mr. Carlton's secretary was speaking firmly to someone.

"The copy room is being used right now. My orders are to make sure that everyone stays out." There was a pause. *"Everyone."*

But the other person wasn't taking no for an answer. "Listen," the voice snapped, "my father's the boss here. He owns the place. So if I want to use that copy machine, I *will* and that's that."

Nancy spun around, the third photo in her hand. Brenda was coming into the room—and there was no other way out!

Chapter

Eight

Brenda barged through the door, slamming it behind her. When she saw Nancy, her mouth dropped open in astonishment, and anger flared in her eyes.

"What are *you* doing here?" she snapped.

Thinking rapidly, Nancy gathered up the photos, standing between Brenda and the machine so that Brenda couldn't see what she was putting into her purse. She turned around.

"My father needed some confidential documents transmitted to New York," she said smoothly. "Your father offered to let me use the facsimile machine."

"Huh," Brenda grunted. Her eyes narrowed. "But what I really want to know is what you were doing hanging around Mike's motel yesterday," she demanded, blocking Nancy's way to the door.

"Mike's motel?" Nancy asked innocently. She pretended to think for a minute. "Oh, yes," she said, "I *did* see you yesterday out on Ridgeview Road, didn't I? Dad sent me out to Mason's Office Supply to pick up some envelopes." She frowned as if puzzled. "You know, the *weirdest* thing happened after that. Somebody came along and smeared lipstick all over the windshield."

Brenda smiled wickedly. "Is that right? I wonder who it could have been." She stepped closer to Nancy and dropped her voice. Her smile was gone. "Listen, Nancy," she said grittily, "where Mike McKeever is concerned, I mean business." Her fingers clenched into a fist. "If I so much as catch you looking in his direction, you'll regret it!"

Nancy could feel the anger rising inside her, but she managed to keep it down. "Don't worry, Brenda," she said, "I wouldn't *dream* of dealing myself into your little game."

She hesitated. Should she warn Brenda that her boyfriend meant business, too—but that he had a different kind of business in mind? No, a warning at this point would only make Brenda even more angrily determined to hold on to

Mike. She might even let him know that somebody was on to him.

Pushing past Brenda, Nancy walked out the
door. She had better things to do than argue with
Brenda. Ned would soon be along to pick her up
for the drive to Silver Hills.

"Something happened this morning?" Ned
asked with a look at her tense face when Nancy
got into his car.

"Yes—something I *didn't* need," Nancy said,
and told him about her encounter with Brenda.
But as they drove through the countryside, she
gradually relaxed, watching the green trees speed
by.

"Well, here we are," Ned said as they pulled
into the little town. "Where to first?"

"According to Brenda, Mike played at the
Sweet Corn Festival here last year." Nancy
pointed to a small brick building. "There's the
Chamber of Commerce. Maybe somebody in the
office could help us." She thought for a minute.
"How about posing as magazine writers, looking
for leads on a story about people who get started
in their music careers by doing festivals?" She
patted her purse. "I've got a photo of Mike
—maybe someone will recognize it."

The small office was empty except for a tired-
looking potted palm beside the counter and a
young woman in her late teens.

"Good morning," she said, coming to the counter. When Nancy gave her their cover story, she accepted it without question. "What an interesting article," she said, smiling. "How can I help?"

Nancy pulled out Mike's photo. "We're particularly interested in this guitar player," she said. "He played in the festival last year. His name's Mike McKeever."

The young woman glanced at the photo. "That's right, but his name's not McKeever. It's Malone—Mike Malone. And it wasn't a music career he was interested in while he was here."

"Oh?" Nancy asked. "What do you mean?"

"Just that he had other things on his mind while he was here—especially Laura Rogers. But for details, you'd have to talk to Laura's best friend Pam. She works at the Beauty Box."

Nancy got Pam's last name, and then she and Ned walked down the tree-lined street. The Beauty Box was a small beauty salon attached to a house. It was painted pink, with purple trim. Inside, the salon was empty, and a pretty, dark-haired girl in a pink uniform was reading a magazine. A bell on the door tinkled when Nancy and Ned came in, and she looked up.

"Did you want an appointment?" she asked, coming to the receptionist's desk.

Nancy shook her head. "Actually we came to talk to you—if you're Pam, that is."

The girl looked at them suspiciously. "I'm Pam. What do you want?"

Nancy held out Mike's picture. "We understand that you may know this person."

Pam looked at the picture and her mouth tightened. "Yeah, I sure do." She frowned. "You're not friends of his, are you? If you are, you might as well get out of here right now. I don't want to talk to you."

"No, we're not friends," Nancy said. Maybe, to get this girl to talk, she needed to prompt her a little. She cleared her throat. "Actually, we're a little concerned about this friend of ours. She seems to . . . well, she thinks she's in love with him."

"Then I have some advice for *her*," Pam snapped. "Tell her to run, don't walk, to the nearest exit. Don't even wait to say goodbye."

"Sounds like this guy's made some real trouble here," Ned said sympathetically.

"You bet he's made trouble," Pam said, sitting in the receptionist's chair. Her voice was bitter. "He breezes into town for the festival and makes a big play for Laura, who was engaged to my brother. She's my best friend." She paused and then gave Nancy a meaningful look. "Correction, she *was* my best friend."

Nancy looked at Pam sharply. "You mean something happened to her?"

"Yeah. She got involved with this Mike and

broke off her engagement with my brother, that's what happened to her. Then her father—he owned the big manufacturing plant just outside of town—heard that she and this guy were planning to elope. So her parents got into the act too."

"What do you mean?" Ned asked.

Pam shrugged and picked up a pencil, turning it over in her fingers. "Nobody knows for sure. People say there was a payoff of some kind, but you know how small towns are. Everybody knows about it, but nobody knows the truth. Anyway, Mike and his buddy left town. Laura got mad at her parents for interfering, and she went to Chicago. And now my brother's eating his heart out for a girl who jilted him for a jerk."

"You said that Mike had a buddy," Nancy said intently, putting the photo into her purse. "Was he an older man? Gray beard, scar on his left cheek?"

"That's the one," Pam replied. "His name's Felix. He was living in a travel trailer."

The bell on the door jangled, breaking the tension. A woman came in. "Good afternoon, Pam," she said. "Are you ready for me?"

"Sure thing, Mrs. Lipman," Pam said. She forced a cheerful smile but her eyes were still darkly bitter. She turned back to Nancy. "I've got to get to work now."

"Of course," Nancy said. "You've been a big

help to us. But one thing more. We'd like to talk to Laura's family. How do we reach them?"

"You don't," Pam said, pulling a pink shampoo cape from a rack. "Her mother's moved away. Her father took it real hard about Laura. They split up, and I don't know where he is now."

"So what's on your mind?" Ned said, reaching for Nancy's hand. "Serious stuff? Angry stuff? We've been back for ten minutes, and you haven't said a word." It was almost five, and Nancy and Ned were sitting in the Drews' den, drinking the tall glasses of iced tea Hannah had poured for them.

"Sad stuff, I guess," Nancy admitted, "and angry too. I was thinking of all the lives these two guys—Mike and Felix—have messed up. There's Laura and her fiancé, who broke up because of Mike, and Laura's folks. And Darla —*she's* mixed up in this too."

"I wonder how many *other* lives have been wrecked by this pair," Ned said somberly.

Nancy shook her head. "Yeah, I wonder. It makes me sick when I think of the way Laura was used. And Brenda, too. I mean, I don't like Brenda, but I *hate* what's happening to her."

Ned squeezed her hand. "You're doing your best to stop it, Nan."

"I just hope my best is good enough," Nancy

said fervently. She sighed and looked out the window. "But with Brenda throwing wild cards into the game, I can't be sure."

The phone rang beside the sofa, breaking into Nancy's thoughts.

"Hi, detective," the friendly voice said on the other end of the wire. "Glad I caught you."

Nancy's fingers tightened on the receiver. "Did you get my transmission this morning, Dirk?" she asked tightly.

"You bet I did." There was a suppressed excitement in Dirk's voice. "We don't have anything on the print yet, but I've got a positive on the photo for you."

"Already?" Nancy exclaimed. "That's super!"

"Your boy was involved here in Fort Lauderdale with a girl named Darla DeCamp," Dirk said. "She was on a missing persons list up your way until a couple of weeks ago." He paused.

"Darla?" Nancy asked. It was the name on the love note in Mike's pocket! They were getting closer. "You said she *was* on a missing persons list. What happened? Has she been found?"

"Yeah, she was found," Dirk said. His voice was grim. "She turned up in a lake outside of Batesville—dead."

Chapter

Nine

NANCY GASPED, HER fingers frozen on the telephone. Darla—dead? This was something she hadn't expected. Had Darla drowned accidentally—or by some other means? Nancy thought immediately of the scented note in Mike's pocket. "I pray that we'll never be separated," the girl had written lovingly.

Nancy bit her lip, her thoughts racing. "Have the police established a cause of death?" she asked, her voice strained.

"Not yet," Dirk said. "The case must still be open—they haven't put out a warrant. Where are you in *your* investigation?"

"I've uncovered a couple of things that connect Mike McKeever to Batesville." Quickly, Nancy told Dirk about the ticket stub and the love note from Darla. "And Ned and I discovered a lead today to a girl in Silver Hills," she said. "It's beginning to look as though Mike's romancing these girls for their money. It's romantic extortion. The question is, what next? Does he murder them to keep them quiet, once he's got their money? What's more," Nancy continued, "I'm pretty sure Mike isn't in this alone. It looks like he's got a partner. His name may be Felix."

"You seem to know more about this case than anybody else," Dirk mused. "You'd better watch yourself. These guys sound dangerous. If they figure you're on to them, they might try to stop you."

"I know," Nancy said. "But it's not me I'm worried about. It's the girl I'm supposed to protect—Brenda Carlton. She's about as flaky as they come, and headstrong, and there's no predicting what she'll do. She's so crazy about Mike, she might even try to help him get away."

Dirk grunted. "Sounds like a tough one, but you're up to it. I'll let you know the minute we turn up anything on that print."

Nancy said goodbye and hung up. Just then the doorbell rang. It was George and Bess, in matching red jogging shorts and red sweatbands.

"Hi," Bess said breathlessly as Nancy opened the door. "We were out running—or I should say George was out running, and I was trying to keep up—and we thought we'd stop to hear what you learned in Silver Hills."

"Did you uncover anything new?" George asked.

"Yes," Nancy said. "But what we found out is pretty grim, I'm afraid. Do you have time to discuss the latest?"

"Listen," Ned said, coming up behind Nancy, "It's getting to be dinnertime. How about something to eat while we talk?"

"That's a good idea," Nancy said, suddenly remembering that she and Ned had only had a quick sandwich for lunch.

"I'll go for that," Bess said happily.

"But we've *had* dinner," George reminded her. "What about your diet?"

"What about it?" Bess asked, with an innocent look. "Don't you remember what we always used to say back in high school? There *aren't* any calories in Hannah's kitchen."

Hannah surveyed the group as they came trooping into the kitchen. "Dinnertime, is it?" she asked, laughing, hands on her hips.

Ned enveloped Hannah in a huge bear hug. "You know, Hannah, I'd sure love one of your terrific grilled-cheese sandwiches and some tomato soup. And your chocolate cake has always held the key to my heart." He grinned at Nancy. *"One* of the keys to my heart, anyway."

"So what happened in Silver Hills?" George prompted as the group sat around the table.

Nancy sketched out what she and Ned had learned from Pam at the beauty salon, and then went on to the conversation with Dirk. Everyone grew quiet when she told them about Darla DeCamp's death.

"But there's no proof that it was more than an accident?" Bess asked.

"Dirk didn't have any information on that," Nancy said.

Bess shook her head. "I keep thinking about that poor girl writing that love note," she said gravely. "What a rotten thing—to love somebody and then find out that he's a crook." Her eyes widened. "If Mike and his friend killed that girl, what are they planning to do with Brenda?"

Nancy frowned. "But we don't know that Mike killed anybody," she said cautiously. "We're only guessing. I think we ought to make a trip to Batesville and talk to the police. Maybe by this time they've got some leads."

The phone rang, and Hannah picked it up. "Yes, sir," she said, "she's right here."

She carried the phone to the table. "It's Mr. Carlton," she whispered to Nancy. "The editor of the *Times.*"

Nancy took the phone. "I'm glad you called,

Mr. Carlton," she said. "I've got some important information to share with—"

"That'll have to wait," Mr. Carlton snapped. "This is an emergency."

"But I need to tell you about—"

"Tell me later. I want you to get out to Flannagan's Farm tonight. I've just overheard Brenda talking to Mike on the phone. Apparently, he asked her to meet him out there, at ten o'clock tonight—alone. I don't want her out there with him all by herself."

Nancy nodded. "Yes, I understand," she said quickly. "It *wouldn't* be a good idea to leave them alone. We'll keep an eye on them all evening. If you want, we'll even put a watch on Mike for the next few days to be sure that Brenda's safe. But I think you ought to hear what I found out today in—"

"I'd like to hear what you've learned, Miss Drew, but I just don't have the time. I've been called out of town for a couple of days on a *very* important business matter. My pilot's taking off in twenty minutes."

Nancy thought. Since Mr. Carlton was leaving, there was no point in telling him about Darla's murder, or the possible payoff Laura's father had made in Silver Hills. "I see," she said quietly.

"I hate to leave in the middle of this thing with Brenda," Mr. Carlton was going on. "While I'm gone, it's up to you to keep a close eye on my daughter. I want her protected, at all costs. And I *don't* want her to know that she's being watched. Do you understand?"

"Yes, sir," Nancy said. Yes, indeed, she thought grimly as she hung up the phone, there *were* certain fundamental similarities between Mr. Carlton and his daughter, especially a tendency to give orders.

"What's up?" Ned asked, finishing his cake.

"We're on night duty," Nancy told him. "We're baby-sitting Brenda at Flannagan's Farm."

Bess looked at Nancy curiously. "Why, that old dairy farm's nothing but a few broken-down barns. What's going to happen out there?"

"Nothing," Nancy replied firmly. "As long as Ned and I are there."

At ten o'clock, Nancy and Ned drove down the lane in Nancy's Mustang. They parked out of sight, on a small knoll overlooking the barn lot.

From there, she and Ned could see the overgrown pastures that had once been a working farm. Poor Mr. Flannagan would have hated to see his farm looking like this, she thought. Before he died, it had been a thriving dairy farm, but now the estate was tied up in a family quarrel, and the place was overgrown with weeds, the buildings tumbling down. It was a favorite parking spot for the local teens.

"Your work brings us to the most *romantic* places," Ned said, glancing out the window. "Look at that moon—and those fireflies."

But Nancy was too busy to pay attention to the full moon sailing through the clouds overhead or the fireflies dancing fairylike through the trees. She had pulled out a pair of binoculars and was scanning the barn lot.

"What did you bring those for?" Ned asked, sitting up. "You're not going to be able to see anything with them at night, especially with the moon playing hide-and-seek."

Nancy handed them to him. "They're night-vision binoculars," she told him. "Extremely powerful ones."

Ned looked through the binoculars. "They really *are* powerful! I can even read the fine print on that sign over there."

"Oh, yes?" Nancy asked curiously. "What does it say?"

"No parking," Ned told her, with a laugh.

Ten minutes later Nancy saw the lights of a car coming down the lane. The single light of a motorcycle bounced after it. It was Brenda and Mike, Nancy saw as the red car drew nearer.

"They're here," Nancy announced, watching through the binoculars. "Brenda's getting out."

Ned squinted through the darkness. "I can't see anything. Now what's happening?"

"Mike's parking his motorcycle," Nancy reported. "Now he's walking over to her. She's kissing him."

After a few minutes, Ned asked, "Now what?"

"She's still kissing him," Nancy reported with a laugh. Suddenly the moon came out from under a cloud and the barn lot filled with silver light. Brenda pulled away from Mike.

"Looks like they're just talking," Ned said.

"Yeah. But he's got one hand on her arm and the other—" Nancy swallowed. "The other's in his jacket pocket, and he's looking around, as if he wants to be sure that nobody sees them." She put the binoculars down. "What if he's got a *gun* in his pocket?"

Ned pulled the binoculars away from Nancy and put them to his eyes. "They're walking somewhere," he said. "Brenda's a step or two ahead, as if she's leading him."

"Or he's pushing *her*," Nancy said, the anxiety knotting her stomach.

"It looks like he's taking her into the barn," Ned said. "Brenda opened a door and they're going inside."

"That settles it!" Nancy exclaimed. She reached for her small but powerful pocket torch and opened the car door. "Brenda could be in serious danger! Come on! We've got to get closer."

Together, Nancy and Ned swiftly made their way down from the knoll and ran toward the barn. They crouched beside the half-open door. The moon had ducked under a cloud and the scene was blanketed in inky darkness.

"I don't hear anything," Ned whispered into Nancy's ear after a moment.

"I don't either," Nancy whispered back. "What do you suppose they're doing?"

They were silent for a moment. The only sounds were the chirping of crickets in the grass. Then, suddenly, there was a low, half-strangled cry from somewhere inside the barn, then another.

"It's Brenda!" Nancy whispered, the goose bumps rising on her arms. "She's in trouble. Mike must be after her. Come on—we've got to get in there and help her!"

Quickly, and as silently as she could, Nancy stepped through the dark doorway. The blackness overwhelmed her, and for a minute, she couldn't see anything. Then, as her eyes got used to the dark, she could begin to make out the outlines of two figures, locked in what looked like a desperate struggle.

"They're over there," Ned whispered, grabbing her arm. "I can just barely see their shadows against the barn wall. It looks like he's got his hands around her throat!"

Chapter

Ten

NANCY TRAINED HER torch on the corner and switched it on. There, in the glare of the light, was Brenda, standing on tiptoe, her arms wound around Mike's neck. She was kissing him passionately, utterly oblivious of anything else.

But when the light hit them, Brenda gasped in surprise. Dropping her arms, she stepped backward, tripped over a bucket, and sat down with a loud *oomph!* in a pile of hay. Mike stood still, shielding his face from the light.

"Who . . . who's there?" Brenda stammered, panic-stricken.

Nancy cleared her throat. "It's . . . it's Nancy

Drew," she said. "And Ned Nickerson." She flicked off the torch.

"Nancy Drew?" Brenda gasped. "What are you doing here?" Her voice rose shrilly. "How long have you been spying on us?"

Nancy's face was red. "I—I . . ." She swallowed. "Well, to tell the truth, Ned and I came out here for a little, well, a little privacy." She laughed an embarrassed little laugh. "We used to come out here when we were still in high school. Isn't that right, Ned?"

Ned slipped his arm around her waist. "Yeah," he said, in a reminiscent voice, "it's always been one of our favorite places."

The moon came out just then, shining through the window. Nancy could see Mike's face. He was watching them suspiciously. Had they tipped their hand? Did he know they were on to him?

"Well, you're not going to spoil *my* evening," Brenda snapped. She reached for Mike's hand. "Come on, Mike. Let's find somewhere where we won't be bothered by sneaks who get their thrills spying on other people."

Mike cleared his throat uncomfortably. "Well, actually, maybe it would be a better idea to call it an early evening, Brenda. I did a late set at Charlie's last night, and I guess I'm more tired than I thought." He glanced at Nancy. "And

I'm sort of out of the mood. I'm going home."

Brenda glared furiously at Nancy as she followed Mike out of the barn. "Just see what you've done!" she hissed. "You've messed things up again! Get out of my life and *stay* out!"

"Whew," Ned said as he and Nancy watched Brenda spin her wheels pulling out of the barn lot, close behind a disappearing Mike. "Well, at least Brenda's safe for the rest of the evening."

"Yeah," Nancy said. "I wish we hadn't jumped in on them so fast, but I really thought . . ."

"I know," Ned said, circling her shoulders with his arm. "But we accomplished what we came for, didn't we? It's really tough to be responsible for Brenda."

"And getting tougher all the time," Nancy agreed. "Tomorrow I'll check with the Batesville police to find out if they've got a cause of death in the DeCamp case. But more important, we've got to keep Mike under surveillance. He's the only one who can lead us to Felix. And by watching Mike, we can be sure that Brenda's safe."

Ned chuckled. "I never thought I'd see the day when *you* were worried about Brenda Carlton!"

Nancy hung up the phone, feeling confused. "Boy, *that* sure was a weird conversation," she said out loud, to the empty living room.

At that moment, Ned stuck his head in through the open door. "What's so weird?" he asked.

"I just called the Batesville police," Nancy replied, still puzzling over the call, which made no sense at all. She picked up her sweater and joined Ned outside. They were using Ned's car for the stakeout because it was unfamiliar to Mike.

"Who did you talk to?" Ned asked as he backed out of the driveway.

"To the chief of police—Saunders, his name is. He sure wasn't very informative. All he would tell me was that the case was still open. He wouldn't even tell me how the girl died. I guess I'll have to make a trip to Batesville and talk to him, person to person."

"Did you tell him you had a lead?"

Nancy nodded, frowning. "Yes, but even *that* didn't seem to interest him."

Ned turned a corner. "That *is* weird—a cop who isn't interested in a lead on a case."

Nancy opened her purse. "But I did learn something interesting from the call. Remember I told you that the old guy made a telephone call from Mike's motel room?" She pulled out a slip of paper.

Ned nodded. "Yeah. Didn't somebody in the telephone company trace it for you?"

"That's right." She held out the slip of paper

so Ned could see it. "When I dialed the Batesville Police Department this morning, I recognized the number. It's the same one that Felix dialed from Mike's room."

Ned looked surprised. "But that's crazy!"

"Exactly," Nancy said. "Why would a crook —if that's what this guy is—call the cops?" She shook her head. "It's totally weird."

Nancy puzzled over the problem all day, as she and Ned sat parked across the street from the Ridgeview Motel, watching Mike's room. But she couldn't even guess at an answer, so she abandoned the puzzle and concentrated on the stakeout.

There wasn't much in the stakeout to concentrate on, either. If it hadn't been for Ned's company, the day would have been so boring that Nancy might have dozed off. Apparently Mike was sleeping late, because he didn't appear until nearly one o'clock, when a pizza delivery man brought a large white box to the door. After Mike paid him, he left. The door didn't open again until early evening.

"There he is," Ned said excitedly as Mike came down the stairs and walked across the lot to his motorcycle.

Nancy tensed. "It's about time," she said. "I was beginning to think the day was going to be wasted."

Mike revved the motorcycle and drove onto

Ridgeview Road, heading out of town. Smoothly, Ned started up, and they followed him, careful to stay out of sight.

A mile down the road, Mike turned in at a shabby trailer park. A neon sign said Vacancy. "Remember what that girl told us back in Silver Hills?" Nancy asked as Ned parked on the street and they got out of the car. "Mike's buddy Felix lived in a trailer. Maybe he's taking us to Felix!"

Nancy and Ned made their way through the main gate, scanning the rows of battered-looking mobile homes parked close together on dusty lots. Near the very back, Nancy pointed to a small travel trailer. Mike's motorcycle was parked out front.

"There's the bike," she said. "He must be inside that trailer."

Swiftly they made their way through the shadowy space between the closely parked trailers. In a few seconds, they were standing just below the trailer's small louvered window. Inside, Mike was talking to somebody.

"You mean that strawberry blonde with the great legs?" he was asking incredulously. "You're crazy, Felix."

"Look." The other voice was exasperated. "Nancy Drew just happens to be a hotshot detective. I read a newspaper story about her and a helicopter crash up in Canada. She not only survived the crash, but inside half an hour she'd arrested the woman who sabotaged the chopper."

"Yeah, but—" Mike said.

"Wait, there's more. I found out that a former mayor of this very town is breaking rocks somewhere upstate because of this girl. He had everybody in this town fooled about a murder for twenty-five years, until she got on the case. She's had more people busted than you've got fingers and toes." There was a disgusted snort. "And you let *her* get a picture of you! That was really *stupid.*"

The silence stretched out. "Maybe we'd better pull out now," Mike offered at last, "before she gets on to us."

"Nah, we're too close. Besides, we need the cash. That job in Batesville didn't pay off the way it should have. Fortunately, there're no mug shots of you, so the picture shouldn't hurt us too much. But Brenda practically gave Drew a road map to everywhere we've been. If I hadn't bumped the table and dumped that coffee in her lap, no telling what else she might have spilled. And now that Drew's got the photo, you can bet she'll take it somewhere where people will recognize you and talk."

"So what's the big deal if she does?" Mike retorted. "So we picked up a a few bucks from some rich kids' parents. Most of them were more than willing to give me that money. And they'd be too embarrassed to say anything about it now. You're making it sound like we're wanted for murder."

There was another long silence. Nancy stood on an old wooden crate and peered through the window. Mike was glaring at the gray-bearded man—Felix—across a small table. There was barely room on the floor for a huge, short-haired dog lying at the older man's feet.

Nancy waited for Felix to respond but he only said, "Look, the way I figure it, we still have a couple of days before Nancy Drew gets enough on us to cause real trouble. That should be enough time for you to sweet-talk the Carlton girl into making her move. Time for me to do my work, too." His voice dropped threateningly. "And don't get involved, like you did with Darla."

Mike laughed harshly. "Felix, you've got to be kidding. Get involved with Brenda Carlton? Not a chance. Yeah, she's pretty, but—"

At that second, the dog lifted its head and growled menacingly. Startled, Nancy shifted her weight and the crate she was standing on collapsed with a crash. The dog gave a low, rumbling bark.

"There's somebody out there!" Felix said in a half whisper.

Ned pulled Nancy to her feet. "Come on," he said, "we've got to get out of here."

Together, they began to run into the darkness at the back of the trailer park. From the sound of the dog's frenzied barking, it had been set loose and was closing in on them.

Her muscles straining, Nancy ran harder, a pace or two behind Ned. But the ground was littered with junk—boxes, old tires, broken auto parts—and she had to weave in and out through the rusty piles. The breath burning in her throat, she cast a look back over her shoulder. The dog was gaining, its lips laid back in a snarl, its sharp teeth gleaming in the dim light.

Then, just ahead in the darkness, Nancy could make out the webby shadow of a tall chain-link fence. If only she could reach the fence, she'd be safe. But behind her the huge mastiff made a giant lunge, his fangs bared. He was just inches away!

Chapter

Eleven

Give me your hands, Nancy," Ned said urgently. He was straddling the top bar of the six-foot-high fence, reaching down.

Nancy held up her hands and Ned grabbed her wrists, half lifting, half dragging her over the top. Nancy felt as if her arms were being pulled out painfully at the shoulders, and below her she could hear the dog, snapping viciously as he jumped for her.

Over the fence, Nancy and Ned faded into the shadows as the mastiff threw himself against the wire, snarling in furious frustration. Felix was a dozen paces behind the dog, a club in his hand.

"Did you get them?" Nancy heard Mike shout as he ran up beside Felix.

"Nah." Felix spat out the word in disgust. "They got away." For a moment he paced along the fence, with the dog sniffing at the wire. Then he called the dog and went back to the trailer.

"Do you think they saw us?" Nancy whispered. They were crouched in the shadow of a dumpster, surrounded by the smell of rotting garbage.

"I hope not," Ned whispered back fervently. They crept out of the shadows and down a dark alley toward the car. Ned unlocked it and they climbed in.

"We really hit the jackpot tonight," Nancy said, ticking off what they had learned on her fingers. "We managed to track Felix down. We know for sure now that he and Mike *are* in cahoots, and that they've been involved with at least three girls—Laura, Darla, and Brenda —and who knows how many more. We know that they had something to do with the Darla DeCamp case in Batesville, and that it didn't pay off the way it was supposed to. And we know that Mike was personally involved with Darla—who is now dead."

Ned started the car and they drove off. "Uh-huh," he agreed, checking the rearview mirror to be sure they weren't followed. "But Mike said something back there that sounded like he knew they *weren't* wanted for murder."

"I heard that too," Nancy replied, nodding. "Felix was telling him how stupid it was for him to let me get his picture, and he said, 'You're making it sound like we're wanted for murder.' I don't think he would have said that if he'd been responsible for Darla's death."

"Well, we still don't know how Darla DeCamp died," Ned reminded her. "Maybe she fell out of a fishing boat." He shuddered. "Or maybe she committed suicide."

"We've got to find out," Nancy said. "Tomorrow I'm going to Batesville."

"Do you want me to come?" Ned asked, turning onto Main Street.

"No, there's plenty to do here," Nancy told him. "We promised Mr. Carlton we'd protect Brenda, and that means keeping an eye on Mike."

"If it's all the same to you, I'll stick with Mike." Ned turned to grin at Nancy.

"Okay." Nancy nodded. "George and Bess can double up on Brenda. It takes two to watch her, anyway. I'll give them a call when we get home."

Ned glanced at her. "Any idea how long it's going to take to wrap this thing up? I seem to remember something about a vacation that got postponed almost a week ago."

Nancy shook her head. "I can't say when this thing is going to end. Somehow, we have to convince Brenda that Mike is only after her money. And we have to get firm evidence that will take these guys out of circulation. We need something so clear that even Brenda can't miss it."

"Just be careful, Nancy," Ned said. "There's something fishy about the way the Batesville chief handled your call. I don't trust him. And it sounds like you're on Felix's hit list already."

"Don't worry—I'll keep my eyes open," Nancy said grimly.

"I'm sorry, Ms. Drew," Chief Saunders said in a flat, expressionless voice, after Nancy was seated in his bare office on Friday morning. "I'm not in a position to reveal any of the details of the DeCamp case—not even the cause of death." He was a ruddy-faced man with chilly blue eyes. Those blue eyes were fixed on Nancy now as he leaned back and folded his hands across his belt. "In fact, I'm wondering why you're so interested in this business."

"I told you over the phone," Nancy said, trying to sound more patient than she felt. "I'm investigating a case in River Heights that involves two men, a younger guy using the name of Mike McKeever and an older one named Felix."

Nancy studied the chief's face as she spoke. Was there a flicker of interest in those cold blue eyes as she mentioned Felix?

Nancy went on. "These two have been involved in a similar case in Silver Hills. And I think they're connected to Darla DeCamp."

"I see." Chief Saunders leaned forward. "And what is your evidence?"

Nancy hesitated. "I found something in Mike McKeever's possession," she said slowly, "with Darla's name on it. And a ticket to the Batesville County Fair."

The chief leaned back again. "I hope you'll forgive me if I say that your evidence isn't very conclusive," he remarked. "What else?"

"I know that Felix made a phone call to Batesville," Nancy said, watching the chief carefully to see his reaction. She could have added "to this number," but she didn't. What if Saunders were involved in this somehow?

"Hmm," the chief said, picking up his pencil. He looked at Nancy and his blue eyes were even chillier. "Well, if you'll tell me where I can find these men, I'll look into it."

"But that's not what I had in mind," Nancy said, frustrated. "I need to find out how Darla DeCamp died."

The chief stood up. "I'm sorry, Miss Drew," he said pleasantly, "but that's the best I can do."

"I see." Nancy stood up too, and cast a mistrustful look at the chief. "Thank you," she muttered, and left.

Well, there's more than *one* way to crack this thing, Nancy told herself as she got back into her Mustang. If the chief wouldn't cooperate, she'd try something else. She stopped at a phone booth and checked the directory. There was a Howard DeCamp listed at 135 Crown Drive.

Crown Drive was on the outskirts of the peaceful little town, and the DeCamp house was at the end of it. The brick house was large and imposing, with a long graveled driveway bordered with roses. It was a house that had been built by somebody who had plenty of money, and it had a peaceful, serene air. But Nancy had the feeling that the peace and serenity were only an appearance. Underneath, there was something else. Darla had lived here, and now she was dead. And Nancy suspected that the last few weeks of her life had been anything *but* peaceful and serene.

Nancy rang the doorbell. After a few minutes, a thin, dark-haired man opened the door a crack. His hair was disheveled and it looked as if he hadn't shaved for a week.

"If you're a reporter, go away," he said gruffly. "I won't talk to you."

"I'm not a reporter," Nancy told him. "My name is Nancy Drew. I'm a private detective from River Heights. I know that this is a very difficult time, but I'd like to ask you a few questions about your daughter, if you don't mind."

The man's eyes narrowed. "I *do* mind," he said, and began to close the door.

"Please, Mr. DeCamp," Nancy pleaded. "I know this is hard for you, but with your help, justice can be done and—"

"Justice!" Mr. DeCamp spat out the word. "My daughter is dead! Justice can never bring her back again! Don't talk to me about *justice!*"

"Perhaps I can help," Nancy said softly. She opened her bag and pulled out the photo of Mike, holding it up. "Can you identify this man?"

Mr. DeCamp stared at the photo, the color draining from his face until it was pasty white. "Yes," he said, swallowing hard. The Adam's apple bobbed up and down in his thin neck. "That's the man who killed my daughter!"

Chapter
Twelve

So she *was* murdered," Nancy said softly.

"Yes, but the police won't admit it," Mr. DeCamp said, his shoulders slumping. He opened the door. "I guess you'd better come in."

Mr. DeCamp led Nancy down a short hall and into a thickly carpeted and elegantly furnished living room that stretched the width of the house. A woman in a burgundy housecoat lay on a velvet sofa, listlessly watching a soap opera on television. On top of the television set was a gold-framed picture of a vibrantly attractive young girl, with soft brown eyes and a dimpled smile. A small bouquet of fresh flowers was arranged beside the picture.

Mr. DeCamp turned off the TV. "We've got company, Emily," he said gently. "This young lady has come to talk to us. Her name is Nancy Drew, and she knows something about—" He cleared his throat. "About Pete Mitchell."

"I don't *want* to talk about that man!" Mrs. DeCamp wailed. She put her hands over her eyes. "If the police won't do anything about him, what can *we* do?"

"Pete Mitchell?" Nancy asked. "Is that the name he was using here in Batesville?"

Mr. DeCamp nodded. He dropped down into a chair and motioned to Nancy to take the one across from him. "What do you know about him?"

"I know that he has a history of duping young women," she said. "He apparently romances them, then somehow convinces them to give him money, and pulls out of town. Your daughter wasn't the first one he conned, but if I wrap this case up quickly, she might be the last."

Mrs. DeCamp sat up. Her hair was tousled and her eyes were bloodshot. "Tell her, Howard," she said urgently. She pounded her fists on her knees. "Tell her *everything*. If she can bring Darla's murderer to justice—"

Mr. DeCamp went over to the woman. "Now,

Emily," he said softly, "you're not supposed to excite yourself. Your heart—"

"Tell her," the woman repeated, lying back and closing her eyes in exhaustion.

Mr. DeCamp took his seat again. "It all began when Darla went down to Fort Lauderdale on a little vacation," he said wearily. "While she was there she got mixed up with Pete Mitchell—the guy in the photograph. He followed her back here and took a job playing guitar at the Waterloo Inn." He rubbed his eyes. "Emily and I tried to convince Darla that she shouldn't waste her time on him. But that only seemed to make matters worse. She'd always obeyed us before, but this time she was determined. She said she loved him." He sat back in the chair and closed his eyes.

"And then what happened?" Nancy prompted.

"Well, the thing went on for a couple of weeks. Then I got a call from some friend of Mitchell's, warning me that Mitchell and Darla were eloping. The caller told me that he could convince Mitchell to leave town—*without* Darla—for a price. It was a lot of money, but I paid it. Or rather, I paid half of it."

"Something happened to interrupt the plan?" Nancy asked.

"Yes. I made the first payment, but then Darla disappeared. For a while her mother and I thought she had run away with this guy, although we couldn't understand why she didn't call us or write to say that she was safe. We were terribly afraid that something was wrong. Anyway, Mitchell's friend never called back, and I never made the second payment." He cleared his throat again. "A few weeks ago a fisherman found her body, in the lake outside of town."

"And she'd been murdered?"

"The police say she'd drowned. But the autopsy showed that her skull was fractured. I think Pete Mitchell knocked her out and threw her into the lake."

Mrs. DeCamp sat up again. "What we can't understand," she burst out hysterically, "is why Chief Saunders won't investigate the case! He keeps telling us that there's no evidence to charge Pete Mitchell and that crony of his, but we think there is! We can't understand why—"

"Emily, please, calm down," Mr. DeCamp said. He turned back to Nancy. "If you have evidence linking this man to Darla—or to any other young woman—it ought to be taken to the authorities. There's got to be somebody else who can act on it, the county district attorney or *somebody*—"

"What about the other police on the case?" Nancy asked. "What's their opinion?"

Mr. DeCamp laughed shortly. "There's only

the deputy," he said, "and he doesn't count. In Batesville, Chief Saunders is the boss."

At that moment, the doorbell pealed sharply.

"I'll get it," Mr. DeCamp said with a glance at his wife, who lay motionless on the sofa. Out in the hallway Nancy heard him open the door. Then she heard a flat, expressionless voice. It was Chief Saunders!

Holding her breath, she went to the door of the living room, where she could hear the conversation.

"—see from the car parked out front that that young woman from River Heights is here talking to you," the chief was saying smoothly.

"Yes, she's here," Mr. DeCamp conceded. His voice rose. "What business is it of yours?"

"Well, now, Mr. DeCamp, it's nothing to get excited about." The chief's voice was conciliatory. "I just thought I ought to warn you that it's not a real good idea to talk to outside people about this business. I mean, we don't know exactly what happened out there at that lake, and until we do—"

"Chief Saunders," Mr. DeCamp said in a firm voice, "I intend to talk to *whoever* will help me bring my daughter's killer to justice. And you can't stop me!" Nancy heard the door slam violently.

"There!" he said, coming back into the living

room. Outside, there was the sound of the chief's car driving off, tires spinning on the gravel. "I feel better already!" He looked at Nancy. "Miss Drew, is there any way I can help you?"

"I think so," Nancy said. "I would like to see the lake where Darla's body was found. I know it will be difficult for you, but it *would* be a help."

Mr. DeCamp glanced toward the sofa where his wife lay. "Let's take my car," he said.

The lake was about five miles out of town, in a heavily wooded area. Mr. DeCamp drove down a rutted road, to a rocky beach. A wooden raft was moored about fifteen yards out from shore.

"It's not much of a lake," Mr. DeCamp said, getting out of the car. "People fish out here, and in the summer the kids swim off that old wooden float." He pointed up the shore about fifty feet. "Her body was found washed up in those trees." He choked. "She'd been dead for three weeks."

"Is it possible that she was swimming out here and hit her head?" Nancy asked.

"That's what the police chief keeps saying," Mr. DeCamp replied. "But she wouldn't have been swimming in the middle of April. And she'd never been fishing in her life. No, there's only one reason she'd come out here—to meet that no-good Pete Mitchell. *He* killed her!"

"Well, I'll do my best to stop the man you think did this," Nancy promised. They drove back to the DeCamps', where Nancy said good-bye, got in her car, and drove to the Waterloo Inn.

The manager, a plump, motherly-looking woman, confirmed that an entertainer named Mitchell had worked there, and that she'd sometimes seen him with Darla and with an older, gray-haired man.

"Such a shame about Darla drowning," she said, shaking her head. "She was such a pretty girl, and always so mannerly. I tell all my kids not to swim at that lake, especially at night."

"So you think she was swimming and hit her head?" Nancy asked.

"That's what I read in the paper," the woman said decisively. "Anyway, everybody knows that lake is dangerous."

By the time Nancy had finished at the inn, the sun was setting into the flat, empty horizon. Nancy drove past the now-deserted town square and turned onto the highway to River Heights. The road ahead was perfectly straight and empty. Nancy rolled down the windows to enjoy the mild evening air.

It wasn't a bad evening for a drive, Nancy thought, checking her watch. She ought to be home by ten. In the meantime she had plenty to occupy her thoughts. There was the police chief's reluctance to pursue the case, for one thing. And the way he had responded when Nancy mentioned the phone call from Felix. It was almost as if he already *knew* about it. But what connection could there possibly be between Felix and the Batesville police chief, unless the *chief* were involved in the case too, and covering up for—

Nancy looked up. The highway had been completely empty, except for a tractor in the distance, but a car—an old one, judging from its silhouette—suddenly pulled out of the rest stop she had just passed. She could hear the squeal of the tires even over the noise of the Mustang's engine. In a half second, the old car had eaten up the distance between them. Was he trying to bump her in the rear?

But the car pulled out to pass, and Nancy relaxed a little. Then she glanced to her left, and what she saw chilled her blood. The car—an old green Buick—had pulled up beside her. There, as close as if he were sitting across the dining-room table, was Felix. He was looking directly at her through the open window, and there was a slight smile on his lips.

Nancy shivered. Felix? What was *he* doing here?

In the second after their eyes met, Felix jerked his steering wheel, sending his car reeling in her direction.

There was only one thing Nancy could do. She hit the brakes and yanked her steering wheel to the right as far as she could, toward the tall corn that lined the road. As she started to throw herself across the passenger seat, she felt the car skidding through the loose gravel at the side of the road.

The next second, everything went black.

Chapter

Thirteen

Victim is a female Caucasian, long blond hair, in her late teens, possible concussion . . ."

Victim? Nancy thought groggily, trying to turn her head. The voice faded out and back in again. Her head hurt, as if someone had hit it with a baseball bat.

". . . driving a blue late-model Mustang, license number . . ."

Mustang? He must mean me, Nancy thought. She fought against the blackness, pushing it away. She was lying on her back with her head resting against something firm and a little damp.

Nancy managed to open her eyes a little.

Everything was hazy, as if she were opening her eyes underwater, and she couldn't move either of her arms. But she could make out a red light flashing some distance away, at the end of a long, green tunnel. After a moment she realized that the tunnel was a narrow path of flattened corn, and that the red light was on top of the police car parked at the edge of the road. A state highway patrolman was giving Nancy's license number into the microphone of his radio.

There was a second voice, from another direction. Nancy moved her head slightly. It was another highway patrolman. "Can you describe the suspect car, the other car that was involved?"

"It was an old green Buick," a third voice said. The speaker was an old farmer in coveralls, sitting on the hood of her Mustang, which was nosed into the corn. "One of them big, ugly green bombs they used to make years ago. Lots of chrome up front. Must've had four hundred horses under the hood. He was doing at least ninety by the time he passed me."

"And where were you at the time of the incident?" continued the second voice.

"I was coming down the side of the road on my tractor, hurrying to get home before my missus got dinner on the table. I saw that Buick pull up beside the gal's blue car and make a quick turn right toward the little gal. And then the blue car went off the road." He pointed dramatically to the path Nancy's Mustang had plowed. "She tore through my corn just like those stunt cars do in the movies."

"What did the suspect vehicle do?" the patrolman asked.

"Well, he must've seen me, because he pulled back into his lane all of a sudden. Came flying past me like he was a jet." The old farmer squinted down at Nancy. "Look, she's coming to."

The patrolman knelt beside Nancy. "It's okay, miss, just lie still. The ambulance is on its way, and you'll soon be—"

But that was the last Nancy heard. Blackness closed over her again. Helplessly, she felt herself falling into it.

It was morning when Nancy woke up again, and outside the window birds were singing cheerfully. The walls of the room were white. The ceiling was white, too, and so was the scratchy gown she was wearing. She turned her head. Ned was sitting beside her, dozing, his head propped up by his hand.

"Ned?" she whispered. "I'm so glad you're here."

With a start Ned came wide awake. "Nancy?" He leaned toward her and covered her hand with both of his. "You're awake? You're okay?" His voice was tense and strained and he looked tired, as if he'd been up half the night.

"I'm awake," Nancy said. "Whether I'm okay is still a big question mark." Slowly, she moved one arm, then the other, then both legs. "Well, at least I can move everything."

"Thank heaven," Ned said fervently. He bent forward and kissed her. "Oh, Nancy, what would I do if anything happened to you?"

"But nothing *has* happened—nothing permanent, that is." Nancy struggled to sit up. She put her fingers to her forehead, where she felt a giant lump. "When did you get here?"

Ned propped the pillows at her back. "Hannah called about nine, and I got here about eleven-thirty. I think I set a land speed record on the interstate."

"Hannah called you?"

"Right. The hospital phoned her to find your family. Since your dad wasn't in town and her car was in the shop, she called me. The doctor said you'd just suffered a mild concussion when you hit your head. You were really lucky. From what they told me, it sounds like somebody tried to kill you."

"Better not move around, young lady," a nurse said briskly, coming in with a breakfast tray.

"But I've got to get out of here," Nancy exclaimed, suddenly remembering everything.

She pulled at Ned's hand. "We've got to get back to River Heights, Ned! Brenda's in real danger!"

The nurse put the tray on the table at the foot of the bed and pushed it toward Nancy. "Not so fast," she said. "You're not going *anywhere* until the doctor says so. Since it's Saturday, he won't start his rounds for a couple of hours yet."

"A couple of hours!" Nancy moaned. "By then it could all be over!"

"It might be over sooner than that if you don't relax," the nurse warned with a smile.

"Calm down, Nancy," Ned said gently. "You'll think better after you eat." When the nurse had left the room, he added, "How about filling me in on everything—from the beginning?"

By the time Nancy had finished breakfast, she had sketched out the events of the day before, beginning with her discussion with Chief Saunders and ending with her unexpected side trip into the cornfield. "The thing I can't figure out," she added, "is how Felix knew I was in Batesville. Unless—" She tried to think, but her head was still aching and it was hard to concentrate.

The door opened. "Good morning, Miss Drew." It was Chief Saunders, in uniform. He took off his brown hat and glanced at Ned. "I'd like to talk to this young lady alone, if you don't mind."

"*I* mind," Nancy told him. "Ned's staying."

The chief shrugged. "Have it your way," he said, watching her with his cold blue eyes. "Are you ready to answer a few questions? I want to know why you went out to the DeCamp place and bothered Mr. and Mrs. DeCamp."

"I needed to know how Darla DeCamp had died."

"And what did you find out?"

"That her skull was fractured, and that she died from drowning."

"And what else?"

"That her parents think that she was murdered —by a guy calling himself Pete Mitchell."

"And you think you know where this Pete Mitchell can be found?"

Nancy folded her arms across her chest. "I thought you weren't interested," she said cagily.

"I *am* interested," the chief said. "I'm going to put my deputy on this case, and I want you *out* of it."

"No way," Nancy said in a low, firm tone. "I have a client's interests to protect, and I have absolutely no intention of getting off this case."

"Miss Drew," the chief said, leaning forward and fixing his eyes on hers, "do you know what a material witness is?"

Wordlessly, Nancy nodded.

"If you don't swear that you'll get off this case, I am going to lock you up. As a material witness to the death of Darla DeCamp."

Nancy looked at him calmly. "I think my father might have something to say about—"

The phone rang. Ned reached for it, spoke into it briefly, and then handed it to Nancy. "It's for you," he said with a glance at Chief Saunders. "It's Dirk Bowman."

"Who's that?" the chief snapped.

"Dirk Bowman is a Fort Lauderdale detective," Nancy said coldly. "He's assisting me on this case. If you don't let me talk to him, he's going to know that something very odd is going on here."

The chief frowned, his ruddy forehead wrinkling. "Well, okay," he growled. "I guess you can take the call. But I'm going down to the nurses' station and listen in."

"Suit yourself." Nancy took the phone from Ned as the chief hurried out of the room.

"Nancy?" Dirk asked. His voice was worried. "You okay?"

Nancy laughed ruefully. "Just a little the worse for wear," she said. "But I'm going to be out of here shortly. How'd you track me down?"

"Your housekeeper told me you'd been in an accident and that I could reach you at the Batesville hospital. Listen, detective, I've got a make on that print you sent me."

Nancy sat up straighter. "Oh, yes? What did you find out, Dirk?"

"The print doesn't belong to your boy, after all."

"Too bad," Nancy muttered. "Now we'll never find out who—"

"Hang on a sec," Dirk interrupted. "The print belongs to somebody named Felix Frankson." His voice was grave. "Frankson is an escaped murderer, Nancy. He's wanted by the FBI!"

Chapter
Fourteen

Wow!" Ned whistled shrilly when Nancy hung up the phone and told him what Dirk had said. "It sounds like this man Frankson has a lot on the line. No wonder he was willing to go after you!"

The door opened and Chief Saunders came in without knocking, his hat in his hand. He stood for a minute in the door, looking at Nancy, his blue eyes carefully guarded.

"All right," he said finally, "I've decided to let you go. Whenever the doctor releases you, you can leave."

Nancy nodded. "Did you hear what Dirk Bowman told me?"

"I heard," the chief said. "I aim to get on this in a hurry." He glared at Nancy. "And I don't want you to try to pull any funny stuff. This is serious business—*police* business. I don't need any kids messing things up." He jammed his hat on his head. "You stay out, you hear? I won't be responsible if you get yourself hurt again."

"Listen, Ned," Nancy said urgently as soon as the chief had left the room. "Mr. Carlton ought to know what's going on. There's no proof, but it looks as if Felix and Mike killed Darla. Brenda could be next. Let's call him at home." She picked up the phone and began to dial.

"Isn't it risky calling the house?" Ned asked. "Brenda might answer."

"You're right," Nancy said. "But it's Saturday, so Mr. Carlton won't be at the office. If Brenda answers, I'll hang up."

But it was the Carlton maid who answered the phone and told them that Mr. Carlton was still out of town. "He's not expected back until later today," she said. "Is there any message?"

Nancy bit her lip, frowning. "No, no message," she said. She had to talk to Mr. Carlton himself.

"The next step," she told Ned as she hung up the phone, "is getting out of this hospital."

"You're *sure* you're okay?" Ned asked. Nancy

could see the worry in his eyes, and she squeezed his hand. It was wonderful to know that Ned cared for her.

"I'm sure," she said confidently. "All we have to do is to convince the doctor."

That was harder than Nancy thought. The doctor came in with an X ray in his hand to tell her that she could go home the next day.

"Tomorrow!" Nancy exclaimed. "That's just not possible. And anyway," she fibbed, "once I get home I'll go straight to bed."

The doctor held up the X ray and looked at it for a long time. Finally he said, "Well, I guess I don't see any real damage. If you'll promise to get plenty of rest, you can go."

"I promise," Nancy said. She *would* get some rest, she told herself, except that it probably wouldn't be right away.

Ned and Nancy drove back to River Heights in Ned's car, leaving Nancy's Mustang in the Ford shop in Batesville for repairs to its front end. On the trip back, Nancy tried to puzzle out the complicated relationships in this case, but after a while she dozed a little, still feeling the effects of the bump on her head.

"Wake up, Nancy," Ned said, shaking her gently. "We're home."

Nancy stretched and blinked, looking at her watch. "It's five. Let's call Mr. Carlton."

But Mr. Carlton was calling *her,* as Nancy discovered the minute she came in the door.

"Nancy, are you okay?" Hannah demanded. She was in the hall, the phone in one hand.

"I'm fine," Nancy said. She nodded at the phone. "Is that for me?"

"It's Mr. Carlton. But shouldn't I tell him that you can't . . . ?"

Nancy shook her head. "This is *important,*" she said. "Mr. Carlton? We have to get together, right away. I've got something very important—"

"I do too," Mr. Carlton said grimly. "Do you know the park on Allegheny Avenue? Meet me there in fifteen minutes—at five-thirty."

"Actually, I'm not supposed to move around a lot," said Nancy. "Can you possibly come here?"

"Are you all right?" Mr. Carlton asked anxiously.

"I had a little car accident," Nancy told him. She decided not to get into the attempt on her life. Mr. Carlton was upset enough as it was.

"I'll be right over," Mr. Carlton promised.

Nancy hung up. "He's on his way," she said to Hannah and Ned. "Now I'd better call George and Bess. I may need them tonight."

When Mr. Carlton arrived, he seemed nervous and preoccupied.

"Is Brenda okay?" Nancy asked.

"Brenda was fine when I left," Mr. Carlton said. "But I think I've just blown everything."

Nancy stared at him. "Blown it?"

"I just got back forty minutes ago. There was a call waiting for me when I walked in, from a man who said he was a friend of Mike McKeever's."

"It must have been Felix!" Nancy exclaimed.

Mr. Carlton shrugged. His eyebrows were drawn together in an angry line and his mouth was tight. "He didn't say his name. But he *did* say that he knew about McKeever and my daughter, and he could fix it—for a price. A *big* price." He looked down. "That's when I blew it."

"How? What did you say?"

"I lost my temper when the guy started talking money. I told him what he could do with his offer." He swallowed, the worry beginning to displace the anger in his eyes. "What's worse, I told him that I'd hired somebody to expose his fraud. I told him that we had enough to put him and his partner away for a long time."

Nancy stared at him in consternation. After a minute, she said, "Well, it's too late now to wish things had been done differently. But now that Mike and Felix have been spooked, we're going to have to act fast." She quickly sketched what she had found out about Mike's relationship with Darla DeCamp and Felix's criminal record.

"Their last victim wound up dead," she concluded. "I think Brenda risks death every minute she spends with Mike."

"I agree," Mr. Carlton said bleakly. "What are you recommending?"

Nancy thought fast. "It's time that we got the River Heights police into the act. Sergeant Tom Robinson is a friend of Dad's. He's helped me out on a couple of other cases. And it's time to confront Brenda with the truth, don't you think?"

Mr. Carlton grimaced. "I suspect that's going to be harder than collaring those crooks."

"But just as necessary," Nancy reminded him.

"Right," he said. "When I left, she was just getting home. We can talk to Brenda, and then you can call your friend on the police force. Are you up to coming with me?"

"I think I can manage—with Ned's help."

Ned and Nancy followed Mr. Carlton as he wound through River Heights' most posh neighborhood, enormous houses set well back from the street behind spacious sweeps of green lawn. The Carlton house itself was a mansion with white plantation-style columns.

"Brenda!" Mr. Carlton shouted as they came

into the front hallway. "Brenda, where are you? I need to talk to you."

There was no answer.

"Brenda!" Mr. Carlton shouted. He took the stairs two at a time, with Nancy and Ned right behind. Upstairs, Brenda's room was to the left. It was a huge room, with French doors that opened onto a private balcony. The bed was heaped with clothes. Brenda's dressing table, littered with makeup, stood in one corner.

Nancy went to the dressing table. There was a note taped to the mirror. She handed it to Mr. Carlton. As he read it, Nancy saw his face go white.

"What is it?" she asked.

"We're too late," Mr. Carlton said dully, thrusting the note at her. "Brenda has run away —with Mike McKeever!"

Nancy took the note out of Mr. Carlton's hand. With Ned looking over her shoulder, she read it aloud.

Dear Daddy,

I am writing this so you won't be worried. The most wonderful guy in the world has asked me to go away with him. Mike is a very talented entertainer, and I'm sure that with a little help from me, he'll be a real star. I know that if I'd told you about this, you would have tried to stop me. I'm doing it this way to make it easier for all of us. I'll let you know when we get where we're going. Don't worry—I *know* Mike will take good care of me.

Love,
Brenda

Chapter

Fifteen

Mr. Carlton buried his face in his hands. "Take good care of her," he repeated hollowly. "Yes—the same way they took good care of Darla DeCamp!"

Nancy glanced around. "It looks as if she didn't take her luggage," she said, pointing to a suitcase still in the closet.

Mr. Carlton wasn't paying attention. "I'd never have believed she'd do something like this without telling me first," he said, almost in tears.

Nancy surveyed the room. A jewelry box lay open, exposing the empty velvet tray. Obviously,

Brenda had grabbed all her jewelry hastily—one garnet earring lay forgotten beside the box.

Ned spoke up. "Maybe we can catch up with them before they get out of town."

"There isn't a moment to lose," Nancy agreed. "We'll cover more ground if we split up. Ned, would you pick up Bess and get over to the Ridgeview Motel? George and I will check out Charlie's and see if they've been there. Mr. Carlton, could I borrow your car? Mine's still in the shop in Batesville."

Mr. Carlton nodded. "Should I come along?"

"No, you stay here. We need a command center. We'll call here as soon as we have anything."

A moment later Ned and Nancy were racing to separate cars. Nancy was glad she'd alerted George and Bess. Every minute counted if they were ever going to see Brenda alive again.

Ten minutes later, Nancy and George, in Mr. Carlton's black Lincoln, pulled up outside Charlie's. George went to check the parking lot in back as Nancy dashed inside.

Even though it was early, the place was crowded and the music was loud. A big sign that said BENEFIT TONIGHT hung over the door. But the stage was empty and Nancy realized that the music was coming from a PA system. There was no sign of Mike or Brenda, and she made her way quickly to the office, where the manager was just hanging up the phone.

"Have you seen Mike McKeever?" Nancy asked.

"Yeah, I've seen him," the manager growled, running both hands over his bald head. "The jerk pulled out just a little while ago and left me holding the bag for tonight's benefit. And now I'm being overrun by his fan club!"

"His fan club?"

"First that dark-haired girl he hangs out with, and now you," the manager snapped disgustedly. "When he told me he was leaving, right out of the blue like that, I told him I wouldn't pay him. He didn't seem to care. He was more worried about me remembering to give his note to his girl-friend." The manager's irritation was growing. "She tore in here just a minute ago, grabbed the note, and took off."

Nancy was beginning to feel alarmed. Unless they knew where Mike and Brenda were headed, they could search all night with no success. "Did you get a look at the note? What did it say?"

"I don't know and I don't care. I'm just glad they're gone. You might check the motel." The phone rang and he reached for it. "Now get out of here! I've got a business to run!"

Just inside the door, Nancy stopped at a pay phone and dialed the Carltons' number. Mr. Carlton answered. He had just heard from Ned.

Mike had already left the motel, Mr. Carlton reported. Ned had stationed Bess there in case Brenda showed up, and was headed over to the trailer park.

"We've drawn a blank at Charlie's," Nancy said.

"Where do you think he's taking her?" Mr. Carlton asked worriedly.

"I don't know yet," Nancy said, trying to keep her voice light. "But we're on our way to check out a couple of possibilities."

"What possibilities?" George asked as they climbed into Mr. Carlton's car.

Nancy threw up her hands. *"I* don't know," she confessed. "Where would *you* go if you wanted to meet somebody without being seen?"

George thought for a minute. "How about the camping area down by the river?"

"Good idea," Nancy said, turning the key in the ignition. "Let's take a look."

But the camping area was deserted except for a couple of tent campers. It was beginning to get dark, and the fireflies were dancing through the dusky shadows along the river.

Nancy sat quietly, considering their options. "Well, we can't stay here on the off chance they might show up." She shook her head, frustrated. Where could they have gone? For a minute she watched the fireflies flickering in and out of the trees. Suddenly something clicked.

"Of course! That's it!" she exclaimed.

"*What's* it?" George asked, staring at her.

"Flannagan's Farm!" Nancy said, starting the car. She pulled out of the park, scattering gravel. "That deserted farm would be a perfect place for Mike and Felix to deal with Brenda."

George's face was pale. "What do you think they'll do to her? Just dump her?"

"No," Nancy said grimly. "She knows too much. They'll have to do something to—shut her up." She pressed the accelerator to the floor.

Ten minutes later they were driving down the lane that led to the abandoned farm. Nancy cut the lights and headed toward the knoll that overlooked the barn lot. Below them everything looked just the way it had when Nancy and Ned had walked in on Brenda the last time.

Carefully, Nancy scanned the barn lot again. She couldn't put her finger on it, but something looked different. There was a dark, boxy shadow behind the barn. As the moon came out, Nancy could see the shape of wheels.

"Look! Over there!" Nancy said excitedly, pointing to the shadow. "That's Felix's travel trailer! It looks like it's hidden under a tarp or something. But there aren't any other cars—that must mean they'll all be along soon." She thought quickly. "George, take the car and get Ned at the trailer park. Pick up Mr. Carlton, too. And bring them back here, fast!"

George nodded. "What are *you* going to do?"

"Check things out down there," Nancy told her. "If our gang shows up, I'll keep them busy until you get back with reinforcements." She slipped out of the car and into the darkness.

Nancy made her way quietly toward the dark, boxy shadow she'd seen from the knoll. It *was* Felix's trailer.

She looked around. No one in sight. She took a deep breath and headed for the barn.

Inside, the light was dim as the moon shone through the window. When her eyes adjusted, Nancy noticed a wooden ladder leading up into the shadowy heights of the loft.

Well, the loft is as good a place to wait as any, Nancy thought to herself, climbing the shaky ladder. Above, a section of the roof shingles had blown away, and the loft was flooded with pale moonlight.

The loft—or at least that part of it that still had a roof—was being used to store hay. It rustled as Nancy walked on it. In the center of the loft, there was a large trapdoor. The door was closed now, and fastened shut with a hasp and a wooden peg, a thick cord tied to one end. It wasn't high-tech, Nancy thought, but it obviously worked. You'd tug on the cord to pull the peg, the trap would swing open, and you could pitch the hay down onto the floor below. Suddenly inspired, she scooped up armfuls of loose, dusty hay and piled them onto the trapdoor. If she needed a diversion, she could open the door and drop hay onto someone standing below.

But Nancy's work was interrupted by the sound of motors. Headlights were crossing the meadow. Quickly, she lay down on her stomach and found an opening in the loft floor that gave her a good view of the barn below.

After a moment, she could hear Brenda's petulant voice. "I don't understand why we're coming back here," she was demanding, over the noise of Mike's motorcycle. A car door slammed. Brenda must be getting out of her car.

"Come on inside and I'll explain it to you." It was Mike's voice. "And bring the money."

Brenda came through the main double doors of the barn. She was wearing dark slacks and carrying a small quilted cosmetics case. She sat down on an overturned bucket and opened the case. In the moonlight, Nancy saw the glint of gold.

"What's this junk?" Mike exploded, staring at it.

"Junk?" Brenda asked, offended. "This isn't junk!"

"It sure isn't cash," Mike said sullenly. "I told you to bring money—enough to keep us going for a couple of years, at least. Breaking into show biz doesn't come cheap!"

"But it was Saturday afternoon," Brenda said,

in a whiny voice. "The bank was closed. And besides, this stuff is worth a fortune." She held up a glittering bracelet. "See those diamonds?" Brenda bragged. "They're all real."

"I don't care how real they are," Mike growled. "They're not worth a nickel if they can be traced."

"Traced?" Brenda asked, in genuine confusion. "But who would want to trace it? The jewelry is mine—it's not stolen. I've got a right to sell it and spend the money any way I please." She laughed lightly. "Don't worry, Mike. I *told* you—I left a note for Daddy. He's not going to bother us. Why don't we just get out of here? On Monday we can sell a few of these pieces and we'll have *lots* of cash. And you can get a job playing—"

At that moment, a third figure—a man —stepped through the barn door. Without a word he struck a match against one of the massive timbers and lit an ancient kerosene lantern hanging on a nail. In its soft, golden light, Nancy could see the sinister smile on Felix's face. There was a small pistol in his hand—and it was pointed right at Brenda.

Chapter

Sixteen

Actually, Ms. Carlton, you're not going to get a chance to help us spend that money." Felix stepped forward and seized her cosmetics case.

"Not going to . . . ?" Fearfully, Brenda looked from Mike to Felix and then back to Mike. She stood up, the bracelet falling from stiff fingers. "Mike, who *is* this guy?" she asked, her voice quavering. "What's he talking about?"

Mike stood where he was, making no move toward either Brenda or Felix.

"There's some rope over there in the corner," Felix said, gesturing with his head. "It's moldy, but it'll do the trick. Get it and tie her up."

"Mike?" Without taking her eyes off Felix, Brenda began to back away from him. "Mike? What's going on here? Don't let him take my jewelry!" She turned to Mike, her voice growing shrill with panic. "Mike, tell me this isn't happening! What's going on here?"

Felix threw back his head and laughed. Nancy could see the scar on his cheek.

"Him? Help you? Brenda, my dear, I'm afraid our friend Mike Johnson isn't the type to mess with somebody who's got a gun. Believe me, under all those muscles there beats the heart of a true coward." His laugh was grating. "Anyway, you're missing the point. He wouldn't help you. We're on the same team. Aren't we, my boy?"

"Mike *Johnson?*" Brenda's voice had dropped to a horrified whisper. She was staring at Mike, but he was looking at the floor. "But that's not your name! He's lying—all of this is a lie!"

Mike took a step toward Felix. "How come we have to tie her up?" he asked. "The plan was just to grab the cash and take off."

"I know what the plan was." Felix's voice was gruff. "But I've changed it. In the first place, she didn't bring cash. She brought traceables." He bent over and picked up the bracelet, appraising it. "Good stuff, but traceable nevertheless. We've got to have a long head start to sell it before anyone gets wise."

Brenda shook her head petulantly, obviously

refusing to accept the truth. "Don't worry, Mike," she said, putting both hands on his arm. "We'll get out of this—together."

"You little fool!" Felix laughed. "You don't think that you're the first girl who's fallen for this guy, do you? I'll give this to him, he's got a way with you women."

"But he loves me!" Brenda cried. Suddenly she launched herself at Felix, her arms flailing, her face twisted with fury. "He *loves* me!"

For a moment Felix struggled with her, using his free arm. Then, with a single powerful shove, he pushed her into Mike's arms.

"Sure, he loves you," Felix mocked. "Just like he loved Crystal. Remember Crystal, Mike, back in Indianapolis? And after that, there was Laura, and then Darla. Sure, he loves you."

Furiously, Brenda turned to face Mike. "Who's Crystal?" she demanded, stamping her foot. "And Laura? And Darla?"

Mike didn't answer.

"They were the last three girls who generously offered to help his career along," Felix told her. "Or I suppose I should say that it was their parents who were the generous ones, when they found out that their sweet, innocent little daughters were about to run away with lover boy here." He smiled at Mike. "There were others, too, weren't there, Mike? But after a while, you forget their names. And their faces."

"But I don't understand," Brenda said in a hushed voice. Her shoulders were starting to slump. "Mike, tell me that this is all some sort of horrible joke! Please, Mike!"

Felix sat down on a hay bale directly below Nancy, still keeping the gun pointed at Brenda.

"Some joke." He laughed. "You see, my dear, we've been playing this little game for quite a while, Mike and I. It's very simple, really. We find a place where kids hang out—young girls like you, who have a lot of money and not a whole lot of sense. Mike's good at his job, convincing a girl that he's in love with her. I'm good at my job, too. I'm the one who convinces the parents that it would be smart to hand over their cash in order to get lover boy out of their daughters' lives. See how simple it is? And if anybody's got second thoughts, who do they complain to? About what? That their daughters were stupid enough to get mixed up with somebody like Mike? Or that they were dumb enough to fall for a payoff scheme?"

"You won't get away with this," Brenda whispered. "When my father finds out—"

"But we already *have* gotten away with it," Felix reminded her, holding up the cosmetics case. "Although I must say," he added, "that your friend Nancy Drew gave us so much trouble that we had to change our plan. But only slightly

—I had to make a trip to Batesville last night, that's all."

"Nancy Drew is no friend of mine," Brenda retorted hotly.

Felix shrugged. "No matter. Anyway, I took care of her last night."

"You did *what?*" Brenda asked, unbelieving. Her voice shook with fear and her face was pale.

Felix didn't answer. He had paused, considering. "And now, Miss Carlton, what do you suggest that we do with *you?*"

Up in the loft, Nancy was watching and listening so intently that she'd almost forgotten where she was. But now she felt a tickling in her throat. The air was filled with hay dust, and suddenly she exploded into a disastrously loud sneeze.

Down below, three faces turned suddenly upward. Felix pointed the gun up, gesturing menacingly. But the loft was dark, and Nancy was sure he couldn't see her.

"Okay! Whoever's up there, you've got ten seconds to come down," Felix shouted, running to the ladder and looking up. "If you don't, I'll let you have it."

Nancy flattened herself against the floor of the loft, her breath coming fast. She had thought of using the trapdoor as a diversion, but since Felix had moved, that wouldn't work. She could make a dash for the hayloft door, but it was thirty feet away and most of the floorboards were in bad shape.

"Do you want me to go up and check it out?" Mike volunteered.

"No, we don't have time to play hide-and-seek," Felix said. "Whoever's up there has heard and seen way too much." He hesitated for a moment. Then he reached for the lantern and began to swing it back and forth.

"Hey, you up there," he said. "See this? In five seconds, I'm sending this up to keep you company." He began to count. "One, two—"

"Okay, okay, I'm coming down." Nancy got slowly to her feet. George must surely have found Ned and be on the way by now. If she could only stall for time, help would arrive.

Below, Brenda exclaimed, "It's Nancy!"

"You're crazy," Felix snapped. "I *told* you I took care of her." He put the lantern down and came over to the foot of the ladder. "You up there—hurry it up!"

Cautiously, Nancy backed down the ladder and turned to face Felix. For a stunned second, Felix stared at her, disbelieving.

"You!" he breathed at last. "I thought I finished you off last night!"

Nancy shook her head. "Oh, no," she said pleasantly, dusting off her hands, hoping that her fear wasn't showing. "I was just a little shaken up, that's all."

Then a thought occurred to her. "Didn't Chief Saunders warn you that I was on my way back?" she added, trying to make her guess sound more like a statement. "He *is* the one who told you I was in Batesville, isn't he?"

Something flickered in Felix's eyes.

"I think I've figured it all out," Nancy went on conversationally. She took a deep breath to quiet her fear. "But I still don't understand why he was willing to cover up both extortion *and* murder." She threw a quick look at Mike.

"He was getting a cut at the start," Felix snarled. "After the girl died, he was willing to do anything to save his own skin."

"Hey!" Mike stepped forward out of the shadows. "What's this about murder? What girl are you talking about?"

"Why, about Darla DeCamp," Nancy replied, turning to face him. "Weren't you an accomplice?" But of course he wasn't, Nancy knew. Back in the trailer park, he'd been the one who made it clear that he'd never *thought* about murder!

"Shut up!" Felix commanded. He raised the gun and held it to Nancy's temple. "You talk too much! It's time to close this case, Detective Drew!"

Chapter

Seventeen

But Mike was staring at Felix. "Darla's dead?" he asked dazedly. "You mean, you *murdered* Darla?"

"Of course I murdered her," Felix told him. "I had to—you were so crazy about her I couldn't tell what you were going to do."

Nancy watched as Mike stood there, hands dangling at his sides. "I can't believe it," he said blankly. "I can't believe she's dead."

"Darla?" Brenda cried. She pounded her fist on Mike's arm. "Who *is* this Darla, anyway?"

"Shut up!" Felix shouted, swiveling to aim his pistol at Brenda. "Just shut up!"

Then, without warning, Mike threw himself at Felix. "You *scum!*" he shouted, enraged. The point of his shoulder caught Felix with a thud in the midsection and they crashed heavily to the floor. Felix's hand slammed against the boards and the gun slid out of sight under a pile of hay.

In an instant Felix had scrambled to his feet. The two combatants circled in a crouch, as Nancy watched, holding her breath. But Felix was smaller and much older than Mike, and Mike's unexpected attack seemed to have knocked the confidence out of him.

"Are you crazy, kid?" he whined. His eyes darted back and forth warily as he looked for the gun. "We're in this together, aren't we? What's the matter with you?"

"So that's why you wouldn't let me go back and talk to her!" Mike shouted furiously. "She was dead! You killed her, that night at the lake! She was dead and *I loved her!*"

With that, he crashed into Felix again, and the two began to thrash furiously on the barn floor. On top, Mike had his hands around Felix's neck and was choking him. Felix's face grew a mottled red as he gasped for breath, trying frantically to pull Mike's hands away from his throat. Brenda stood still as a statue, her hands clenched, her eyes blazing with anger.

Nancy glanced upward. The two were directly

beneath the trapdoor. And there on the wooden post right next to her hand, the cord was looped around a cleat. With all her might, Nancy yanked the rope, freeing the wooden peg from the hasp. Up above, the ancient hinge screeched and the door fell open, releasing the hay and burying the struggling pair. Over in the corner Nancy's eye caught a sudden flicker. The lantern! The hay had fallen on the hot lantern and caught fire!

"Come on, Brenda," Nancy cried, grabbing for Brenda's hand. "Let's get out of here! This whole place is going to go up!"

"No!" Brenda came suddenly to life. "I'm not going! I want to see Mike get what's coming to him! After what he did to me, he deserves to get beaten to a pulp!" In the corner the hay began to crackle and blaze.

Nancy reached for Brenda's arm. "I said, let's get out of here," she gritted, between clenched teeth. With one hand on Brenda's back and the other still holding her arm, she hustled Brenda toward the barn door.

"Let me go!" Brenda screeched. "Let me go!"

Somehow Nancy's shoving got the two of them safely through the door. Only then did Nancy release her grip on Brenda, who collapsed in a heap on the grass, sobbing hysterically.

Nancy looked up. Brenda's jewelry was still in the barn, but they'd have to try and get it out later. Behind her, flames were beginning to flicker through the windows. But down the lane she could see headlights—one, two, *three* pairs of headlights!

"Here! Over here!" Nancy cried, jumping up and down and waving her arms.

The lead driver turned on a siren and a flashing red light as the column of cars broke into a line and raced three abreast across the meadow. The cars on the two flanks roared ahead of the third, a black Lincoln. The car on the right, Ned's car, headed straight for Nancy and screeched to a halt in the barn lot. On the left a River Heights police car executed a perfect fishtail skid and stopped just short of the barn.

"Nancy! Are you okay?" It was Ned, piling out of his car with Bess and George.

But Nancy was running toward the police car. Sergeant Robinson jumped out of one door. From the other sprang a young man dressed in a dark suit, white shirt, and tie. "Where are they?" he shouted, jerking a snub-nosed revolver from a shoulder holster.

"In the barn!" Nancy yelled. "Hurry—the place is on fire!" As she turned, the whole side of the barn erupted in a searing belch of flame and black smoke.

But at that moment Mike came through the barn door, silhouetted against the orange flames. He was shoving Felix ahead of him. Felix threw up his arms to shield his face from the glare of the headlights.

Instantly, the young man lifted his gun. "FBI!" he barked. "Hold it right there, both of you! Frankson! You're under arrest!"

Felix fell forward onto his knees. "I've had enough," he groaned. "Don't let him hit me again!"

Nancy stepped forward. "The young guy," she told the FBI agent, "is Frankson's accomplice in a local extortion attempt." She had to raise her voice over the crackle of the flames. "He's also a suspect in other extortions—and possibly an accessory to murder."

"I have a fugitive warrant on Frankson," the FBI agent said, turning to Sergeant Robinson. "Do you want to hold the kid?"

"I want him held for extortion!" Brenda said, her face twisted with fury. "Throw the book at him!" She turned on Mike. "How could you *do* such a thing to me?" she spat at him. "How could you—"

"That's enough, Brenda!" Mr. Carlton grabbed her arm. "It's all over now. Leave him alone."

The two men were searched and handcuffed, and Sergeant Robinson and the FBI agent led them toward the police car. Behind them the burning roof collapsed with a loud roar and a shower of sparks.

Suddenly Brenda shook off her father's arm and ran up to Mike. "I *hate* you," she screamed. "I hate you, I hate you, I—"

"I'm sorry, Brenda," Mike muttered, head down. "I didn't mean for it to end this way."

But Brenda wasn't listening. She turned to her father. "Daddy, I want him to pay for this. I want him locked up for the rest of his—"

Mr. Carlton grabbed Brenda around the waist and began to pull her toward the Lincoln. "One more word," he threatened, "and I'll cut off your allowance for a whole year!"

Chapter

Eighteen

Smiling, Nancy lay back on her beach towel and surveyed the vast expanse of grass and trees in the Carlton backyard. In the swimming pool, George and Bess were batting a big orange ball back and forth across a net. Ned was lying on his stomach beside Nancy, enjoying the warm sun.

"At last," he said, reaching happily for Nancy's hand. "We can get back to our interrupted vacation."

Mr. Carlton came out onto the patio beside the pool, wearing white slacks and a white shirt.

"Sorry I was delayed at the paper," he said to Nancy. "But I'm glad that you and your friends could come over and enjoy yourselves." He sat down in a chair beside them. "After all you've done for Brenda and me, a small pool party seems the *least* we can do for you."

"It's not exactly a *small* pool party," Nancy remarked, glancing at the table loaded with gourmet delicacies. If she ate another ounce, she wouldn't be able to get into her jeans when it was time to go home.

"Speaking of Brenda," Ned said, "where *is* she?"

Mr. Carlton grinned. "Well, that's the reason I'm late." He handed Nancy a typewritten page. "This was written by a certain junior reporter that I believe you're acquainted with."

Nancy began to read the page out loud to Ned.

MOST-WANTED CRIMINAL BROUGHT TO JUSTICE

On Saturday night, after a long and hazardous undercover investigation, a staff reporter of *Today's Times* revealed the whereabouts of Felix Frankson, an escaped murderer known to be very dangerous—

With a gasp, Nancy stopped reading.

"But that's not what happened," Ned said hotly.

"You're absolutely right." Mr. Carlton's grin broadened. "As editor, I had to deliver a rather stern lecture to this particular junior reporter and remind her that fiction has no place in responsible journalism. In fact I insisted that the piece be completely rewritten, with *strict* attention to the facts. I'm afraid Brenda will be delayed—until she gets it right."

Nancy smiled. "Well, it's good to see that she's managing to get over her crush on Mike Johnson."

"So *that* was his real name, huh?" Ned asked, rolling over onto his back and putting on his sunglasses.

"That's right. Sergeant Robinson asked me to come to the station this morning to make a statement. It looks like Mike will plea-bargain for a five-year suspended sentence in the De-Camp extortion. It doesn't look like he was involved in Darla's murder." She turned to Ned. "Remember that comment we overheard him make in Felix's trailer? 'You're making it sound like we're wanted for murder.' For me, that was a giveaway, and later, in the barn, it was clear that he didn't even know that Darla was dead."

"Still," Ned objected, "a five-year sentence is pretty light."

"Yeah, but I got the whole story from Dirk Bowman, and it's pretty sad," Nancy told him. "Mike was a teenage runaway. He knew the real Mike McKeever was dead, so he took his name, knowing that no one would find him that way."

Nancy took a deep breath and continued. "Then Felix picked him up in New York and tricked him into his first con job. After that it was easy for Felix to blackmail him into going along with the other extortions, by threatening to turn him in."

"And now he has to live with the knowledge that his actions led to the death of the girl he loved," Ned said quietly.

Nancy nodded somberly. "Personally, I think that may be punishment enough."

"I agree," Mr. Carlton said. "That's why I've decided not to press charges in Brenda's case. But what about Felix?"

"Felix is going directly back to jail—*without* passing go," Nancy replied.

At that moment the Carltons' maid appeared at the patio door. "Pardon me, Mr. Carlton," she said. "A Mr. Perkins is here. He's looking for Ms. Drew."

"Please show the gentleman out here," Mr. Carlton replied.

The young man who appeared on the patio, looking out of place in his suit and tie, was the same one who had collared Felix the night before.

"I'm Special Agent Perkins," he said with a smile. "I'm on my way back to the field office in Chicago and wanted to stop by and thank you for your help. We've been on Frankson's trail for quite a while, but he's always eluded us." He turned to Nancy. "You really did our job for us, Ms. Drew. I congratulate you on your fine detective work."

"Thanks," Nancy said. "But what about Chief Saunders? What's going to happen to him?"

The agent looked grim. "Chief Saunders was arrested in Batesville this morning and charged with obstruction of justice and aiding an escaped felon. The DA thinks he can build a case of criminal conspiracy in the death of Darla De-Camp as well."

"That should keep him out of action for a while," Nancy said.

Perkins stood to leave. "Well, thanks again. If I can ever be of assistance to you in any of your cases, please let me know."

"Hey, who was that?" Bess asked as she and George climbed, dripping, out of the pool. "He was kind of cute."

"Watch it," Ned cautioned in a teasing voice. "You don't want to get mixed up with the FBI."

"How *did* the FBI get involved?" George asked. "I mean, that guy just seemed to drop in from nowhere."

"It does get complicated," Nancy admitted. "When Dirk Bowman couldn't identify the thumbprint I sent him, he passed it on to the national crime center in Washington. When the FBI made the identification, they got my name —and Brenda's, as well—from Dirk."

"Oh, I see," George said. "So then the field office in Chicago sent Agent Perkins here to pick up Felix."

"Right. Perkins immediately got in touch with Sergeant Robinson. When the two of them couldn't find me, they headed over here. They arrived just as you called Mr. Carlton to alert everybody that we were at Flannagan's Farm. That's why they were in on the grand finale."

Bess spread out her towel beside the pool. "Have you called Dirk yet to tell him that the case is finished?"

Nancy nodded. With a grin she recalled Dirk's warm words of praise over the phone that morning. "Well done, detective. If you ever want a *real* job, give me a call and we'll get you into our police academy."

The door to the patio opened. "Well, is everybody having a simply *terrific* time?" Brenda asked sarcastically.

"Just a minute, young lady," Mr. Carlton said, in a warning tone. "Don't you think you should be a little more polite? After all, if it hadn't been for Nancy and her friends, you might still be in some *very* serious trouble."

Brenda dropped down onto a chaise longue. "Now, Daddy"—she pouted—"that's just not true. I know you don't believe me, but I was on to those crooks from the very beginning. If I'd just had a little more time, I would have wrapped this case up all by myself. I *certainly* didn't need Nancy Drew."

Mr. Carlton looked stormy. "Brenda," he cautioned, "you know what I said about stretching the truth. Now, you *thank* Nancy."

Brenda made a face. "Well," she said grudgingly, "I suppose you helped a *little,* Nancy. But just wait until next time! I'm as good a detective as you are!"

Nancy suppressed a giggle. "Sure, Brenda. I don't need any more thanks."

Brenda stiffened, then stomped away from the group. "I'll show you, Nancy Drew," she flung over her shoulder. "I know my way around —*aaaaaagh!*"

Brenda had tripped over a chaise longue. She teetered for a moment, arms windmilling, then fell into the pool with a *splosh!*

Everyone went running to the edge of the pool. Nancy grinned at her friends. "Come on," she said. "Time to save Brenda—*again.*"

Nancy's next case:

Nancy, Ned, Bess, and George find tropical beauty —and constant danger—when they go to Hawaii. Millionaire bank owner Alice Faulkner has asked Nancy to locate her only grandchild, Lisa Trumbull, who has vanished, taking with her the valuable contents of the family safe deposit box.

Too late, Nancy tracks down the seedy hotel where Lisa had been hiding and discovers that her bills had been paid for by the Malahini Corporation, a mysterious company that no one knows anything about.

Nancy suspects that Malahini is controlled by a traitorous top executive at Mrs. Faulkner's bank. With herself as bait, Nancy lays a deadly trap for the ruthless Malahini Corporation, in *SINISTER PARADISE*, Case #23 in The Nancy Drew Files™.

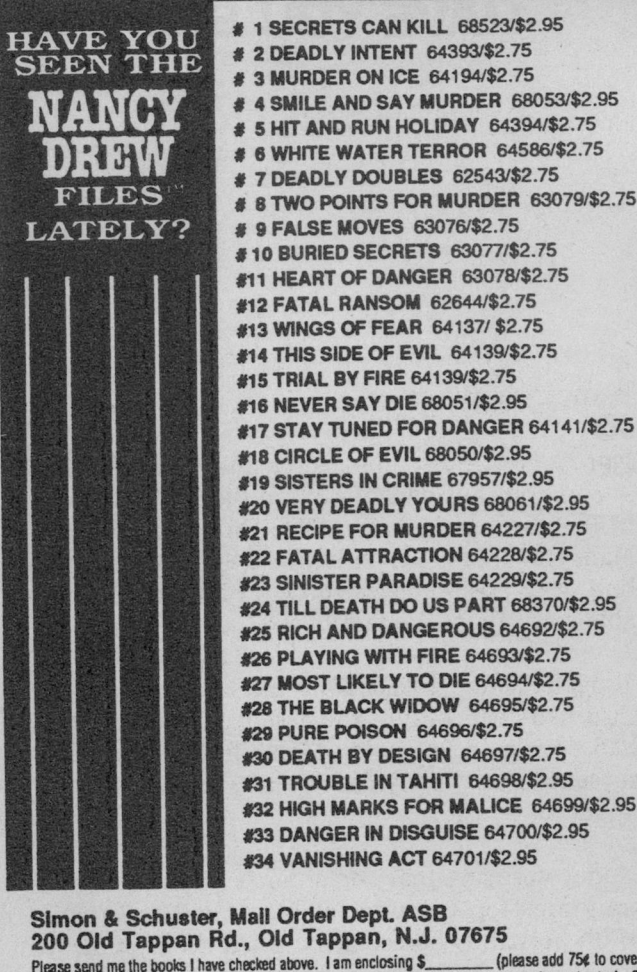

HAVE YOU SEEN THE HARDY BOYS® LATELY?

THE HARDY BOYS©

CASE FILES

- #1 DEAD ON TARGET 68524/$2.95
- #2 EVIL, INC. 67259/$2.75
- #3 CULT OF CRIME 67260/$2.75
- #4 THE LAZARUS PLOT 68048/$2.95
- #5 EDGE OF DESTRUCTION 62646/$2.75
- #6 THE CROWNING TERROR 62647/$2.75
- #7 DEATHGAME 62648/$2.75
- #8 SEE NO EVIL 62649/$2.75
- #9 THE GENIUS THIEVES 68047/$2.95
- #10 HOSTAGES OF HATE 63081/$2.75
- #11 BROTHER AGAINST BROTHER 63082/$2.75
- #12 PERFECT GETAWAY 68049/$2.95
- #13 THE BORGIA DAGGER 67956/$2.95
- #14 TOO MANY TRAITORS 64460/$2.75
- #15 BLOOD RELATIONS 64461/$2.75
- #16 LINE OF FIRE 64462/$2.75
- #17 THE NUMBER FILE 64680/$2.75
- #18 A KILLING IN THE MARKET 68472/$2.95
- #19 NIGHTMARE IN ANGEL CITY 64682/$2.75
- #20 WITNESS TO MURDER 64683/$2.75
- #21 STREET SPIES 64684/$2.75
- #22 DOUBLE EXPOSURE 64685/$2.75
- #23 DISASTER FOR HIRE 64686/$2.75
- #24 SCENE OF THE CRIME 64687/$2.75
- #25 THE BORDERLINE CASE 64688/$2.75
- #26 TROUBLE IN THE PIPELINE 64689/$2.95

Simon & Schuster, Mail Order Dept. ASD
200 Old Tappan Rd., Old Tappan, N.J. 07675

Please send me the books I have checked above. I am enclosing $_____ (please add 75¢ to cover postage and handling for each order. N.Y.S. and N.Y.C. residents please add appropriate sales tax). Send check or money order—no cash or C.O.D.'s please. Allow up to six weeks for delivery. For purchases over $10.00 you may use VISA: card number, expiration date and customer signature must be included.

Name _____

Address _____

City _____ State/Zip_____

VISA Card No. _____ Exp. Date_____

Signature _____
_____120-15